Just as Mother was closing the screen door, a wild screaming came from up the road. I might have thought it was an animal if the voice hadn't been screaming Daddy's name.

"Ezra,Ezra!"

Daddy and Sterling raced down the porch steps. When the screaming got closer, I could see it was one of Daddy's miner friends, Mr. Murphy, with a big rope around his neck.

"They've killed them, every one of them!" screamed Mr. Murphy.

"What are you talking about?" Daddy asked.

"They shot all of them miners going to work the number four. They were going to hang me but I ran away."

"Who shot them?" Daddy lifted the noose off Mr. Murphy's neck and put his arm across the man's shoulders.

"The union men! Nobody I knew. Must have been those men sent to organize."

"Sterling, get my gun, and run over and tell Addie Henderson to get the sheriff."

Sterling kept staring at the noose Daddy held in his hands.

"Don't just stand there—go, boy!"

ALSO AVAILABLE FROM DELL LAUREL-LEAF BOOKS

DAUGHTER OF VENICE, *Donna Jo Napoli*

SHABANU: DAUGHTER OF THE WIND
Suzanne Fisher Staples

DR. FRANKLIN'S ISLAND, *Ann Halam*

COUNTING STARS, *David Almond*

GODDESS OF YESTERDAY, *Caroline B. Cooney*

ISLAND BOYZ: SHORT STORIES, *Graham Salisbury*

SHATTERED: STORIES OF CHILDREN AND WAR
Edited by Jennifer Armstrong

THE LEGEND OF LADY ILENA, *Patricia Malone*

MIDNIGHT PREDATOR, *Amelia Atwater-Rhodes*

UP
MOLASSES
MOUNTAIN

Julie Baker

Published by
Dell Laurel-Leaf
an imprint of
Random House Children's Books
a division of Random House, Inc.
New York

Visit us on the Web! www.randomhouse.com/teens

Educators and librarians, for a variety of teaching tools, visit us at
www.randomhouse.com/teachers

ISBN: 0-440-22903-0

RL: 5.7

Reprinted by arrangement with Wendy Lamb Books

Printed in the United States of America

February 2004

10 9 8 7 6 5 4 3 2 1

OPM

To my father, James Bailes,

whose stories filled my imagination,

and to my mother, Judy,

whose love is boundless

Acknowledgments

I wish to express my heartfelt thanks to my husband, Jonathan, whose many words of encouragement were my source of strength, and to my editor, Wendy Lamb.

I would also like to thank my many friends and neighbors who offered their thoughts and support: Susan Bash, Jamie Bailes, Deborah Ghosh, Jamie Martin and Marina Primorac, Linda Fink and Rick Young, Lucy and T. Weymouth, Maya Primorac, Carolyn Bailes, Bob Belton, Carol and Numa Jerome, Todd and Susan Lowry, and Tricia Beisler.

UP
MOLASSES
MOUNTAIN

Chapter 1

If I'd had a dog, I wouldn't have kicked it. I would have let it walk with me to school and back. It would have kept me company and warned me of dangerous things in the woods like bears and rattlesnakes. Instead, all I had was a chicken. She followed me around and let me scratch her head. She was really one of my mama's laying hens, but I named her Red Baron anyway. I played with her when I had nothing else to do. But what I really wanted was something to call my own, something that heard my voice above everyone else's and came to me when I called it.

I was sitting beside the henhouse when my pop came outside. He looked at me a long while.

"It ain't normal for a boy your age to be playing with a chicken," he said. I shoved Red Baron off my lap and looked at the dirt.

"Well, can I have a dog then?"

"A dog? Why, a dog would only eat your chicken. Besides, I don't spend my days down in that filthy mine to feed no dog."

I pushed myself up and moved toward the porch. Red Baron followed me until I picked up a rock and threw it near her.

"Get away. Scat."

I didn't need nothin' else to make me different from all the other boys. I knew Pop didn't like me much on account of me not being "right." That's what he said when he thought I wasn't listening. I don't know why he bothered trying to hide his opinion from me. No one else seemed to care if I was listening or not.

The kids at school had been calling me retard or slug or something worse all my life. Just 'cause I looked funny and couldn't get my words out as fast as other kids. No one ever bothered with me unless it was at my expense. Groups of girls withdrew to little circles like roly-poly potato bugs when I came around. The boys had fun pushing me into them, thrilled by their squeals. But the fun went out of that game by about fourth or fifth grade. That's when they stopped noticing me at all.

I spent most of the time at school by myself. Even the nice girls, the ones who often gave our teacher flowers they'd picked on the way to school, couldn't bring themselves to speak to me. They'd turn their faces away faster than a hummingbird's wings flap when I caught them staring. They couldn't help themselves. My own pop was much the same way. I kept my head down if he took me anywhere so as not to embarrass him. I always kept my mouth shut, 'cause if people didn't notice my face, they'd sure look twice when they heard the twisted sound of my voice. I didn't want him to be ashamed of me, but he was. The only time I remember my pop being really happy was at the circus.

A year after we'd gone to the circus, I still remembered it like it was yesterday. Circus people were like no people I'd seen before. Their faces were strange and foreign and stayed in my dreams for months after.

"Come on, Clarence, I'm taking you to meet your new family. Get in the car!" Pop had teased that day. It wasn't like him to tease. There weren't nothin' Pop said that he didn't mean.

"Where are we going?"

"It's time for supper," Mama protested from the front porch.

"Put the supper away, Rosemary," he told her.

She stood on the porch with her hands on her hips, completely puzzled. His wide grin spread its way over his face. He was tall, and powerful enough to change Mama's whole mood with one look. "We're going to the circus."

When Mama smiled, I knew it must be true.

"Yippee!" I yelled.

I'd been studying the posters for weeks:

The Russell Ramey Circus
1952 North American Tour
Coming to Clay, West Virginia
We'll dazzle you
with elephants, lions and clowns
when we roll into town.

In our part of Appalachia, most people were miners and didn't have a lot of extra money for shows and things like that. But that didn't keep us from dreaming about it. The week before, I had been swinging on every wild grapevine I passed. I mastered a flip in the hayloft. Only a handful of kids I knew got to go to the circus, but everyone talked about it like they had been a thousand times.

Before I knew it, I was tucked between Mama and Pop in the truck. A line of cars and trucks stretched clear through town. Mama spied her cousin all the way from Braxton County three cars up. She leaned out of the car and yelled, "Anna Mae, it's Rosemary. Are y'all going to the circus?" I don't know where else she thought they were going. I had never seen my mama holler before, except at the chickens.

"Why is the circus coming all the way to Clay?" I asked. The circus usually performed only in big cities like Charleston and Huntington.

"Mr. Bagby is trying to throw us miners a bone," Pop answered. Most of Bagby's miners lived in Widon, deep among the hills with no flat land around. The circus had to set up just outside of Clay where the Elk River took a turn. Mr. Bagby, who owned the mine, had sent a train to bring in his miners who lived in the company town. It wasn't but seven miles, but when they got off the train, they were hooting and hollering like they'd come from England.

Mama's lips were red with lipstick and she smelled like the drugstore makeup counter. People looked at her and she smiled and nodded as we walked to the tent. I never thought of her looking pretty until then.

The air inside the tent was heavy with the smell of sawdust and animals. A couple of clowns took our tickets and one gave my mother a paper flower. She turned her smile toward Pop.

The show began with elephants marching on parade. Each one held the tail of the one in front of them. They sat up and begged like dogs. But the dogs looked more like little girls. They were wearing fancy dresses and walking on their hind legs. The most amazing part of all was the people on the trapeze. They flew out over the crowd, doing twists and turns to every drumroll, falling perfectly into each other's grasp. I wished I could do that. *"And now, Clarence Henderson will perform his amazing double flip."* The crowd would ooh and ahh to the rhythm of each swing, their eyes following my every move.

At the break in the show, Pop came back with three big whips of pink cotton candy. I saw him slide his arm around Mama and give her a squeeze while she pulled pink tufts to her mouth. It was the best day of my life.

Chapter 2

"Elizabeth, look, there's that crazy Clarence again," Hattie said, sitting as still as she could while I braided her hair. Clarence ambled along the edge of the road out in front of our house.

"He's not crazy," I said, "just his face didn't come out right. You should thank God that he gave you all the pieces to your face and all this long blond hair." Not like mine. My hair was plain brown, like dirt that isn't good for anything but mud pies.

"Well, I think anybody who walks around all day by himself talking to animals isn't quite right," she said.

"Maybe the animals talk back to him. Some people know what animals are thinking."

"He talks to animals because he doesn't have anybody else to talk to," she said.

"Hi, Clarence," I shouted from the porch.

He did what he always did—kept looking down

and walking fast, bobbing and weaving among the branches that hung low along the edge of the road.

"It's because he's so ugly, he's afraid he's going to scare you," Hattie said.

"Hush." People said a hare had crossed Clarence's mother's path, causing him to be born without part of his lip. If you looked at him from the back, you might think he was pretty, with hair that curled up a little. But his legs, long and thin, didn't quite fit on his small body. His eyes were the color of a calm summer sky. I tried to stare at them when I talked to him instead of at his mouth, but my eyes drifted down like a moth drawn to light. His mouth had been stretched like cowhide by the doctor who stitched it together when he was born. He lisped because of it, like he had a mouthful of rocks he couldn't spit out.

"He doesn't have any angel's fingerprint on his lip," said Hattie. "I think he got born too early, before the angel had time to make him right."

"You shouldn't say mean things about Clarence," Mother said. She and Grandma were sitting on the porch listening.

"I'm only saying what's true," Hattie said.

"True or not, some things a person just doesn't go around saying," Mother answered.

"Why did God allow him to be born that way?" Hattie asked.

"Remember, God made all of us. I don't know why he made you with your soft hair and Elizabeth with her deep green eyes or Clarence the way he is, but in Jesus' eyes he is as beautiful as anyone and I never want to hear you say otherwise." She paused and looked at each of us full on.

"I didn't say he was ugly to Jesus, I said he was ugly to me," Hattie answered.

"Well, what's good for Jesus should be good enough for you."

"He is pitiful, Mother," I said. "You should hear the boys tease him."

"People are cruel, Elizabeth. That's just the way it is. Clarence will learn to cope with it and he'll be stronger for it."

"But they're so awful to him. They call him half-wit."

"You have a good heart, Elizabeth. Be nice to Clarence now, both of you," Mother said.

Mother was a strong woman, and we did what she said. She wore her auburn hair in a knot, which made her look older than most people's mothers. At night, she would take it down and let it fall over her shoulders and onto her long white nightgown. When I was small, I would sit by the fire watching her hair shimmer as the flames danced. I thought she was the most beautiful woman in the world. People said I looked like her. But I didn't want to look like the Ellen Braxton they knew, with her hair pulled back and her manner firm. I wanted to look like the woman who sat by the fire at night with her hair down.

Chapter 3

Hattie and I were still clearing the dishes off the table when we heard a pounding on the door.

"Who is it?" Mother asked.

"It's Clarence. My mother sent me over to see if you heard the siren."

We rushed out to the porch to listen. It sounded like the low howl of the wind and it flooded our hearts with fear. The siren signaled something wrong at the mine, a collapse, an accident. The mine was two hills and a hollow away. You had to cross a creek, a bottom and the side of another hill to get there. We closed our eyes and lifted our heads to the hills, not wanting to hear but straining to just the same.

"There it is," Sterling said.

My brother was seventeen. When he was younger, he would beg to run up on the hill and watch the fire trucks or ambulances come. Now that he knew what it all meant, he stood quiet with the rest of us, thinking about the men who might be hurt.

"Go on inside now." Mother broke the silence. "There's chores to do."

We marked time by the sirens. Each mine accident lived in our memories fresh as Christmas and Easter. Last fall, it had been our neighbor Mr. Jordan who was killed. The summer before that, it had been Avis Sampson, son of Mr. Sampson, who owned the store.

Mother mended, cooked, swept and did most anything to keep from sitting and waiting. When she was waiting she was idle, and when she was idle she could worry, and when she worried she let fear come in like the cold wind under the front door. So Mother mended, but the rest of us watched as trucks headed up the road.

Sterling's green eyes were fixed out the window. I watched as he tossed his head every few moments to keep his unruly black hair from obscuring his view. Clarence leaned awkwardly against the windowsill, careful not to crowd Sterling. He had never been inside our house before, even though he lived only a stone's throw away. Had he ever been inside anyone's house but his own? He ran his hand back and forth along the window frame, gripping the wood between his finger and thumb.

"I think I'll ride up with one of the trucks to see what happened," Sterling announced.

"I could go with you," Clarence said. Sterling looked away.

"I don't think either of you boys need to be getting in the middle of whatever trouble they have there," Grandma said. Relief flashed across Sterling's face.

Sterling and I used to be best friends. When we were little, Mother said we were like twins, never wanting to be separated. I could look at his eyes or the way his mouth twitched and know exactly what he was thinking, and he could do the same for me. He knew if I had had my feelings hurt at school. I knew when he was upset about not making the football team. When one of us was hurt, we'd sit together on the edge of the porch until we felt strong enough to get up again.

Hattie had gotten older and broken the spell between us. There wasn't anywhere we could go that she didn't want to come along. She didn't have the sense to be quiet, and Sterling didn't have the patience to wait for her. I didn't blame her; she was five years younger than me and acted like she felt she had missed something and had to catch up. The last couple of years, it seemed Sterling had forgotten all about the closeness we shared. But I missed it. I could still read him, and I knew he didn't want to go up on the mountain with Clarence by his side.

"Sit down," Mother said to Clarence.

"Yes ma'am." He hesitated. "Maybe I better go check on my mama."

"I expect it won't be long before their daddy will come to tell us what happened and you can take the news to your mother." He nodded and eased himself down on the couch beside Sterling.

I watched Hattie stroke our kitten's ears while we all waited for the porch to rattle like it did when Daddy scraped his boots. We all jumped up when we heard that sound. He shuffled through the door, his face black with dust. There were washrooms at the mines, and he usually showered before he came home. But not today.

"Was it Red? Was it Red Olson?" Hattie said.

"I wish it was Red, honey. But it isn't."

Red was a legend, the luckiest miner in the world, some said. He'd been trapped more than any miner we knew but had never been hurt.

"There are three men missing—O'Donnel, Patterson and Simpson."

"Three!" Mother had grown up with most of the miners. Losing anyone was like losing a member of her family. But all I cared about was that Daddy was standing there safe.

"Was it a gas leak?" Sterling asked.

"No, it's that dadblamed Hensley. He skimped on the timbers and moved too much coal without buttressing the shaft."

"My pop always says that Foreman Hensley cares more about tons loaded than men," Clarence said. Daddy nodded.

13

"I'm going back to help dig them out. The machines done about all they could do. The rest has to be done by hand. Sterling, you get the hogs in."

"I will."

Daddy wrapped his arms around Hattie, then me. He squeezed me to him. "You be good, like you always are. And I hope to see you all in the morning."

Clarence was standing back against the wall watching. He looked away, and I could tell he was afraid, like me, that Daddy had come to tell us goodbye, just in case.

"You go tell your mama that your pop is going to be with me and I'm going to look after him. You tell her that," Daddy said to Clarence. He jumped up and we watched them go out the door.

Digging a man out of the mine was every miner's duty. Sometimes as many men were lost in the rescue as were in the accident. But there were usually more volunteers than there was equipment. All the men knew that had it been another moment, it could have been them, their wives home crying, their babies losing a daddy. Daddy had said, "Some men volunteer to go every time, men who almost want the walls to come down so that they can be remembered for something."

After a while, Clarence came back to wait for news. He stretched out on the floor and watched the fire with us. Grandma dozed until Sterling woke her with questions.

"Why does Daddy have to be a miner anyhow?"

Grandma stirred and shifted in her seat. She smoothed the sides of her hair and pushed it into the knot that rested just above her neck.

"Your daddy does what he has to do to feed the likes of you."

"I wish we lived in California or Texas or somewhere where they ain't got no mines," he said.

"Then there'd be something else to worry over, some molasses mountain to climb," Grandma answered.

"If you lived in California, you'd have to worry over an earthquake," I said, laughing.

Grandma said, "Way before they began mining coal, they pulled down the biggest trees for logs. Plenty of men died under the weight of them."

"When did they start mining?" Sterling asked.

"Thirty years ago, Mr. Bagby rode all the way from Boston to the heart of West Virginia to seek his fortune in the logging business. He ended up starting the coal mines and building the company town."

The fire was just a few red embers when Daddy walked in, still covered with black coal dust except for a wide white grin.

"Those devils done crawled out the back shaft and came around just when we were ready to give up. They're bruised a bit and wanting of fresh air, but all right."

"Praise God," Mother said.

"Amen to that," I said.

Daddy looked over at Clarence.

"Your pop should be home soon too."

I ran to throw my arms around Daddy, laughing to feel the coal dust on my face.

"Look," I said, turning to show them.

"My turn!" Hattie cried, pushing me away.

"Your mother needs a hug too." Daddy smiled at her over Hattie's head and she blushed.

"Oh!" I said. "Where's Clarence?" We all looked out the door, where he had disappeared into the moonless night.

Chapter 4

The next day, Elizabeth Braxton smiled at me when I walked past her at school. She didn't say nothin', just smiled. I knew almost all the kids in the tenth grade.

I had been with them ever since I was eight, when Mama made the principal let me come to school. He said I was retarded and would be a big distraction for the others since I couldn't talk right. Mama kept me home when I was little so she could teach me my numbers and letters. When I learned those, she said that proved I wasn't retarded. They finally let me come to school in third grade. Mrs. Grayson, the teacher, thought I wouldn't pass, but I did.

Mrs. Grayson looked as mean as she was, with heavy orange rouge on her cheeks and thick gray hair. She sat Henry and me in the corner and told us, "I mean to keep an eye on both of you troublemakers." Henry Fulton didn't come to school much and never did any work. When Henry got in trouble, I got paddled too. He once threw a wad of paper and hit Mrs. Grayson right on the top of the head. I looked up to see her scowling in my direction. She reached down to grab my shirt collar and took me out into the hall. Everyone laughed and stared at me, most of all Henry. But I knew better than to tell. Henry had some big friends, and Mrs. Grayson's paddling was nothing compared to what his friends would do to me if I squealed.

I managed to make it to the tenth grade without flunking once, but Henry didn't even know what grade he was in anymore. I hated school as much as he did, but my mama made me go anyway. In all my days at school, I didn't remember anyone smiling at me the way Elizabeth did. Hers wasn't like the smiles Mama's friends gave me, where their eyes watered a bit and they patted my head. It was just a regular smile, like you might give to someone if they handed you a piece of pie. I thought about it all the way home.

The sun was hot against my back and made me think of the cool water in Lily Creek, just a few miles up the road from our house. I knew I'd feel like swimming after I finished weeding and watering the garden. I grabbed the rusty handle of the pump outside and cocked it a few times until water spewed out. I worked as fast as I could, trying to avoid Pop, who'd holler at me to do something else if he saw me.

I leaned in the kitchen door and reached for a few

molasses cookies leftover from Mama's church meeting, put them in a sack and headed for the swimming hole. I saw Mama watching me from the corner of her eye, but she pretended not to notice.

The nearest creek was the Buffalo but it was black from washing coal. I had to go farther up to swim. To my mind, Lily was the nicest creek in all of Clay County, with crystal-clear swimming holes that held bass. You could see them dart under the rocks when the water was still. It was out of the way for late in the afternoon, so I was surprised when I saw Elizabeth and Hattie walking ahead of me.

Their hair, tied in ponytails, swung like pendulums when they walked. Hattie kicked at rocks and sticks, stirring up dust along the road. They didn't know I was behind them until Hattie looked back.

"You going up to the swimming hole, Clarence?" she hollered.

"I was heading that way."

"It's Sally Jenkins's birthday and Sterling and his friends are going to throw her in." Elizabeth stopped to wait for me.

I didn't really want to go to the swimming hole if a bunch of Sterling's friends would be there.

"Sterling says he can do a flip off the old rope swing," Hattie said, "just like the circus people do on the trapeze."

I had done a flip off that old rope swing a dozen

times. Maybe I could show them something for a change.

"Well, don't just stand there," Hattie said. "Are you coming or not?"

"I reckon." We cut down the side of the bank.

"Look who's here," Sterling shouted. "Hattie and Elizabeth and their boyfriend!"

Elizabeth shouted, "Shut up, Sterling."

Sterling was sitting on the big rock, close to Sally Jenkins and her friends.

"Y'all come on, but don't be expecting me to watch you all the time," he told us.

I was happy to see that Sally's bathing suit was dry and her ribbons tied. Soon they might have something else to talk about.

"Who's going to be the first to swing the ropes?" someone asked. They had thrown the rope over the tree limb several times to make it higher than usual. There were other guys there, older than me. John Beasley, the big football player, said, "Let that idiot try." I felt my face get hot but I pretended not to hear him. Their voices blurred in my head.

I followed Elizabeth as she stepped easily out onto the rock bridge that led to where the bathers sat. I tried hard not to think about leaving.

"Come on, half-wit," Sterling said. The girls around him laughed. "I bet you can't swim anyway. I might have to save him," he said, looking at the girls.

I knew I could swim better than Sterling. I wasn't

20

afraid of that old rope swing, but I couldn't muster the words to answer him.

"Mother said we have to be nice to Clarence no matter how ugly he is," Hattie said, and made the girls laugh even more. The rock where I stood was slippery with green algae and I slid into the creek, dropping my sack of cookies. Everyone was laughing except Elizabeth.

"Poor dog," Irv said, "his supper is all wet."

"You all hush up," Elizabeth shouted. "Stop it!"

The cookies were floating away, so I waded in, grabbed them and made my way back to the bank. "Look," someone said, "he's going to eat them anyway!" I scurried up the bank, found the road and ran, kicking up the dirt.

At Bagby Field, I hopped on the tracks. I sat down by the edge of the track and laid my face in my hands and cried. I hadn't cried in front of anyone since sixth grade.

The whistle from an oncoming train blew when it saw me. But I wanted it to run me down. It would serve them right. Then they'd be sorry. Then they'd cry and wail and say they never meant it and that they were really my friends. My head was ringing; the train rattling kept getting louder and louder until the whistle blew again. I jumped off the tracks and into the thicket on the hillside, feeling the hot steam of the engine hiss at me for my recklessness. When I caught my breath, I reached my hand up to the steel track. It was burning hot.

I cut a path up through the thickest piece of woods, where the blackberries grew and blossomed with the spring's first fruit. The air was damp and cool there. The pines grew too thick for the sun to shine through, thick enough for piles of red needles to cushion the ground. I walked through the trees, breaking the dead limbs, ducking under the lower branches until I reached the top of the rocky hillside. Below me lay the tracks and a tipple where a few men worked. They were the lucky ones, getting to load the coal into the railroad cars, not having to crawl into that pit.

Many times before, I had sat for hours up on that hill, counting the train cars going by and seeing where they'd come from, wondering where they were going. The coal might fire up some shoemaking factory in Toledo or run a steam engine clear across the country. I dreamed of climbing on top of one of those mounds of coal. I might have just then if one had been passing by.

Directly across the hillside was old Devil's Backbone, a narrow road along the top of the hill. Whenever we drove on it, Mama shut her eyes. She shut her eyes when we crossed the swinging bridge too.

The rocks pushed out over the hillside, and when it rained, I could crawl underneath them to a small cave I'd discovered following a fawn's tracks. The ground stayed dry and soft. I could see down to the mine below and across the hilltops. I had carved a hole in the sandstone and buried a tin I had found in the dump. It was not much bigger than a Spam can, but it was much nicer and the lid still closed tight.

I kept the Indian-head coin Uncle Lem had given me

in the tin, along with my rabbit's foot Pop got when he was hunting last Thanksgiving. I had been wanting a snow-white rabbit's foot as long as I could remember 'cause it brought good luck.

When I got it, I wrapped my hands around the soft white fur, closed my eyes tightly and made a wish. I was careful not to tell anyone my wish. I even slept with the rabbit's foot on my upper lip so its power could be even closer to the affliction. But my wish never came true.

The foot lay in the tin alongside my cracked looking glass. My mama had taken down the mirror in the bathroom. When we went into town, she talked and asked questions as we passed storefront windows so I wouldn't see myself or so she wouldn't see me looking. Did she think I wouldn't discover the truth?

I stared at my mirror.

"Ugly half-wit," I said. I hated myself for running, for being like Jimmy Walsh, the boy with the clubfoot. He had come to Clay a few years back with his pop, who worked on mining equipment. People teased him so much that he had to go to Indiana to live with his aunt.

"They don't mind clubfooted kids in Indiana," he said.

I'd never let them do that to me. They had made me run and I hated them for it. I was stupid to let them. I got one more look at my mouth and reeled my arm back. With all my might, I hurled that mirror down the hillside as far as it would go.

Chapter 5

When we returned from the swimming hole, the laundry waved like welcoming flags. We had to duck underneath rows of white sheets to get to the front porch. When we were little, Sterling and I played tag beneath them. Mother complained of our dirty hands grasping the edges of the sheets to hide. She did laundry six days a week and rested on the seventh, like the Lord, she said. Hattie and I each had four dresses: a church dress, two everyday dresses, which we wore to school, and a summer sundress, which we wore every day all summer long. In the evenings we'd wash it out and hang it up to dry.

"Can I do my chores after supper?" I asked.

"I suppose."

I wanted to get as far away from Hattie and Sterling as I could. They had no right to be so cruel to Clarence.

"Thanks, Mother." I ran into my room.

I kept my diary underneath my mattress. I used to

keep it under my pillow, but I knew Hattie had been reading it, so I moved it. I had moved it before from my desk drawer to my pillow when Sterling first discovered it. Our house was so small that we knew all the hiding places.

My teacher Mrs. Anderson had given it to me when I graduated from the ninth grade last year. It was the prize for being the best writer in my class. She said, "You put things eloquently and you can make people think about things in a whole new way." She wrote in the front, *To Elizabeth, May your words find a place here to hold your memories forever.*

With my diary in hand, I headed toward the hills as fast as I could.

"Hey, where are you going?" Sterling hollered from the porch.

"Nowhere."

He jogged up to me. "Why do you always do that?"

"Do what?"

"Run off to nowhere."

"Maybe I like to."

"Oh, you're just mad 'cause I called Clarence a retard. I was just teasing."

"He didn't think it was funny," I said.

"Why are you so worried about Clarence anyway? Do you like him or something?"

"No! I just don't think it's right to tease him."

"Can I walk with you a ways?" It wasn't like Sterling to ask my permission to do anything.

"If you want to."

"Guess who was asking me about you?"

"I don't know." I walked on, pretending not to care.

"Okay, if you don't want to know then I won't tell you."

"Tell me." I turned around.

"John Beasley."

"John Beasley? What did he want to know?"

All the girls were crazy about Johnny because he was on the football team and was real handsome when he combed back his black hair. The very mention of his name made my heart swell even though I had never really thought of him before. He wasn't a boy someone like me would ever think about.

"He just asked me if you were courting anybody," Sterling said.

"What did you say?"

"I said you like Clarence Henderson."

"You've got to be kidding."

"I saw you looking at him the other night. He was definitely looking at you."

"He was not looking at me and I was certainly not looking at him. You didn't really say that, did you?"

Sterling laughed.

"Tell me what Johnny Beasley said."

"Do you really want to know?"

"Tell me!"

"He said you were kind of pretty, that's all."

"He did?"

"He said he was sick of Sally and Angela following him around all the time."

I couldn't help smiling. A couple of boys had liked me in the second grade, but that didn't count. I thought some boys were cute, but I never talked about it except in my diary. When my friends talked about boys, I just listened. I wouldn't dare tell them what I thought, not the way they kept secrets.

Johnny Beasley thought I was pretty? Mama stroked my hair, but even she didn't talk about me being pretty.

Sterling kept on walking beside me. My mind was going over everything at the swimming hole. Had I said anything to him? What had my hair looked like? I couldn't remember.

"I wanted to talk to you about something," Sterling said.

I turned to look at him.

"It's about Daddy and the mines."

"What about them?"

"There's talk about a strike coming," he said. "I've thought a lot about it and I'm going to be a union man."

"Daddy would never let you do that!"

He looked at me hard.

"Besides," I went on, "you only work a couple hours a week. You'll be going off to school next year anyway."

"Who says we're going to be able to afford me going off to college?"

"Mother's been saving for college, and Mr. Bagby's got that fund."

"But I still don't know if it's enough. If the union comes in, Daddy will make more money. We won't have to scrimp and save every penny all the time just to make ends meet."

"Daddy says the union men are nothing but trouble."

"That's just because he's full of those war stories about the communists. He thinks they're practically the same thing as the unions."

"Why?" I asked.

"I guess it's because the communists started off telling everybody they were going to help the people fight against the rich leaders."

"And the unions tell people they're going to help them fight against the mine owners," I said.

"But the communists turned bad. Men like Joseph Stalin took away people's rights. So it's not the same thing. The union men want to give us rights," Sterling said.

"What kind of rights?"

"I heard tell that if the Clay County mine goes union, men will get money when they get too old to work. It's called a pension. And if, God forbid, a man died, his family would get that money. Don't you remember what happened to the Jordans? Neville had to quit school after ninth grade to go to work after his daddy died."

"Why would the unions do that for us? Doesn't it cost money?"

"The union money comes from dues members pay, so it'd be our money. The union is just a group of miners that work together to get leverage to argue for the things they need, like pensions and better wages. Daddy's been down in those mines so long, he can't see straight. He's worked for Mr. Bagby for so many years, he doesn't know the new way of doing things."

"Oh, and you do?" I almost laughed. "But Mr. Bagby has been pretty good to us. He gives an extra bonus for each of us at Christmas," I said. "I don't think Daddy would go against him."

"I know how loyal he is. It's just that he ought to really think about what the unions can do. I just want to see people's lives get better. I want to fall asleep listening to something other than Daddy's cough."

"Unions can get rid of miner's cough?"

"No, but they can get us more money and respect."

I wandered away, turning over what he'd said. Daddy was proud of his loyalty to the company, and Sterling's union interest would feel like a betrayal. I didn't want to think about it. I wanted to think about Johnny Beasley asking about me.

I walked over the hill to the south side, where the

sun spent most of the day and dried the ground. The trees showed no signs of moss and the wind had twisted the trunk of a giant oak until it looked like a chaise lounge. The branch of another pointed to the ground like the leg of a ballerina. I climbed to a sandy spot beside a large rock. From there, I could see blue-green hills meet the soft blue sky. The hills beneath me seemed further away than the clouds.

It was never quiet on the mountain. Some people talked of going there to rest, but I didn't find it restful. Ants crawled over my legs and crows sat atop the highest branches calling out their victories.

My mind was never quiet there either. I brought my diary to capture my thoughts. Sometimes the words poured out so fast I could scarcely write them down.

A lot of times, I wrote about things I'd only heard about. I wrote about the Second World War and what it was like for those who died, about the letters that went unanswered and the dreaded telegrams that came. I wrote about the love that was lost and the love that was born again when a soldier returned home.

I was only five in 1945, and my memories of the war were the earliest I could recall. Everyone worried that we might be a target for German bombs because our coal was a major source of America's power. Mama taped black paper on the windows, which made the house dark in the daytime. She volunteered as a plane spotter during the day and would take Sterling and me with her to the highest hill to look for any German plane that might be overhead. She seemed so brave.

Even though the grown-ups were scared, I loved that time. Everything we did seemed important. Even Sterling and I could go to the dump to help find metal for the war effort. It was all anyone talked about. With the war over, there was nothing left to replace that sense of purpose. Was that what Sterling wanted, something to make him feel important? Did he really believe the union men's promises or just in being a part of something bigger? I wanted to know that feeling too. There was something solid inside me, like the stone inside a cherry. Even though no one else could see it, I felt it there. Maybe Sterling was like me. He wanted something to test his mettle, to help reveal what he didn't know about himself.

There was a hill on the other side of the hollow where the remnants of a gate stood. The house it guarded had burned down long ago. It was a pretty spot up on the hill but away from the creek, so no one took over the place. It would have been hard toting water up that hill, but it would have been worth it for the view, if you cared about such things. Mother would have never lived there; Daddy either. But someday I might.

I wrote about the woman who I imagined had lived there. The way I pictured her, she was strong and beautiful and spoke some European language. She'd come to tame that spot for a home.

I couldn't imagine a life where I couldn't come up on the hill to get away, where I would be living life like Mother, full of family and chores, with no room for time alone in the woods. I suspected I was meant to be a spinster, like Grandma's sister who lived in the woods all her life and only came to town to teach school and go to church.

So why did my heart flutter at the news that John Beasley had paid me mind?

Chapter 6

It was Saturday and I woke up relieved. No school. The day stretched before me and I mulled over what to do. My thoughts gravitated to the dark aloneness of a picture show. I had a host of secret places in the woods where I could go to be alone: my cave, a hulled-out undergrowth hidden along the railroad tracks, the cleft of my favorite treetop. I could whittle away an afternoon watching the red ants tear leaves to build their nests. I might have near died in one of those places and no one would ever have found me. I didn't want that kind of aloneness. I wanted to hear voices. I wanted to see people, but I didn't want them to see me.

"Mama, can I go to the picture show today?"

"How many times do I have to tell you, Clarence? No!"

"But I heard there's a new western with Gene Autry."

"I don't want you around crowds of people," she

said, going over to the stack of magazines she kept piled in a corner of the living room. "Here it is, the picture of that poor boy with polio in the iron lung. You don't want to catch it and be in one of these for the rest of your life, do you?"

"I guess not," I answered.

"You'd never go to another picture show again, once you're in one of these."

"But no one in Clay has polio!"

"There are plenty of kids in Charleston with it. It's only a matter of time."

I jumped off the porch and started walking. The chance of becoming a gimp wasn't worth taking. Instead of the picture show, I'd just walk to the dump. Henry might be there. He hung out there sometimes, looking for stuff among the trash.

Like most of the other kids at school, Henry lived in the company town of Widon, which Mr. Bagby had built a long time ago when he started the mine. Mr. Bagby'd bought up the land all around here. He built the mines, the town, a clubhouse and a baseball field. In Widon there was a restaurant, a drugstore, a post office and a store where you could use only scrip. Scrip was special money that miners got paid. They could only spend it in certain stores, which kept the miners and their families from taking money outside the company town.

The houses in the company town were lined up side

by side. Each one had a porch in the front and a garden out back. My pop said he wanted his own place, where he could do what he wanted without anyone telling him what to do. In Widon the company rules said they had to paint all the houses red on account of Mr. Bagby being color-blind. Red was the only color he could see. The houses were so close together that if you sneezed, someone in another house would say God bless you. Mama said you couldn't expect much more than that for only a few dollars' rent.

I could hear the ping of rocks hitting tin when I rounded the bend in the road. Henry was sitting on a mound of old tires, throwing rocks at an abandoned deep freeze. "What are you doing up this way?" he asked.

"Just walking. What are you doing?"

"None of your business."

"Do you want to shoot some marbles or something?" I said.

"Why would I want to play with you, Henderson? I got better things to do."

"Like what?"

"Guess where I'm going next week?"

"Where?"

"To the circus. Mrs. Bagby is giving me a ticket. She came down and promised my mama a ticket for all of us kids."

"The circus! My pop says one trip is enough. It's the

35

same old tricks every time anyway," I said, but I couldn't really hide my excitement. Pop wouldn't like it if I asked Mrs. Bagby for anything, but the circus was different.

I raced home, except for a few tries at walking the rails and swinging on the vines just up the hillside. One old wild vine was so tall that I could swing nearly thirty feet over the side of the hill before I let go. I liked practicing landing on my feet or doing a roll like I was in the circus. I couldn't stop thinking about it even at supper. I had made a little platform with my knife and was busy rolling a sweet pea to the edge when Pop yelled at me.

"Clarence, how many times do I have to tell you to stop playing with your food?"

"Why, Clarence, I've never seen you act this way before. Put that knife down and use it like you're supposed to." Mama smiled when she said it, and I could tell she wasn't really bothered.

"I'm going to the circus this year," I said.

"We ain't going this year," Pop answered.

"I am."

"Are you sassing me, son?" Pop put down his knife and fork.

"No sir, but Henry said Mrs. Bagby is giving all his brothers and sisters tickets."

"Well, you ain't taking nothin' from her."

"But Pop, she said she could give them to kids who couldn't afford to go."

"That's charity and we ain't taking it."

"Sarah told me that Mrs. Bagby's Christian

Women's Club was sending some kids to the circus," Mama added.

"I wish they'd mind their own business," Pop said. "Ever since Mrs. Roosevelt came here, West Virginia is the popular place for the do-gooders."

"Oh, Addison, don't be so stubborn. The Christian Women's Club did right by Mr. Sanders when he hurt his leg last fall. All his boys got new coats for the winter, and they surely needed them too. You'd think differently if you busted your leg and couldn't work."

"That's another good reason why we need unions, not people like Mrs. Bagby handing out charity."

"Now, Addison, Mrs. Bagby is a model woman for this town by deed and by dress. Didn't you see her beautiful hat?"

"By dress! All those expensive clothes are bought and paid for with the sweat of us miners," Pop said.

Mama looked down at her plate.

"Get yourself a job," Pop said. "Then you can do whatever you like. Till then, you get your orders from me."

"Addie," Mama said gently, trying to calm him, "I've been hearing talk about the unions coming to town. I thought Mr. Bagby paid his miners more than the union miners get. Why would those union men come here?"

"There's more to work than just a paycheck. Unions are the future. Why, Mr. John L. Lewis is likely to come here to Clay himself, seeing that Bagby's mine is the only one in the whole of West Virginia that isn't union. Lewis said it's the number-one target of the United Mine Workers."

"Who is Mr. John L. Lewis anyway?" I asked.

"You don't know anything, do you, boy?"

"Addison," Mama scolded. She turned to me. "Mr. Lewis is the head of the union, the one causing the trouble. I hope you're not going to be involved in it, Addie," she said.

"I'll have to be."

"There might be shooting. I couldn't stand to see you get hurt."

"I don't think you want to see me get walked on either," he said. "It's like this. You shovel all day down deep in the mountain, breathing in dust, and just when you feel like you're learning a job and doing it well, the foreman will up and move you. Nothing you can do about it. Fifteen years, and I may as well be working the birdgang," he said. The birdgang was the lowest of all the mining jobs, for boys just old enough to work: hauling garbage, digging toilets, loading rock dust.

"Unions level the playing field between me and people like Mr. Bagby," Pop said. "They give us miners some clout." He put on his hat and went out the door.

Chapter 7

"Wake up, Hattie," I said, my eyelids heavy with sleep and my bedsheet still tight around me.

"Is it time to get up already?" She yawned. I had fallen asleep thinking about Johnny Beasley. Why had he asked about me when Sally and Angela were so much prettier? I closed my eyes to imagine the faces of the other girls when they saw him talking to me.

"Girls, get your church dresses on. We barely have time for breakfast," Mama yelled from the kitchen. I sat up and looked at my dress hanging on the door. It was faded from two years' wear, with the hem let out twice. "At least Johnny won't be there," I muttered.

"What did you say?" Hattie asked.

"Nothing." I didn't realize I'd spoken aloud.

"Who's Johnny?"

"Nobody. Mind your own business."

"You said 'Johnny.'"

"Come on, girls. Your breakfast is getting cold."

"Elizabeth is dreaming about some boy," Hattie answered.

"You leave Elizabeth alone and come eat your breakfast."

Practically everyone in Clay went to the big Baptist church in town—everyone except the coloreds and the Catholics, who had their own churches. But we went to the small country church down the road. The pastor was a miner during the week and a preacher on Sundays. There weren't any boys my age there except Clarence, no one I cared about looking nice for. My heart was free to feel the power in the music and the Scripture.

I heard God's voice when we sang hymns like "Amazing Grace." I imagined the sea captain who had written the words, broken and repentant, turning his boat around to return his cargo of slaves to their home. I clung to the joy of God's presence as we sang, "He walks with me and he talks with me and tells me I am his own." But that Sunday the preacher was worried more about mining than he was about walking with God.

"Give to Caesar what is Caesar's," he preached. I was daydreaming and Hattie was swinging her feet until we were roused by Daddy's loud "Amen!" Most Sundays, Mother had to pinch Sterling to keep him awake. But not this Sunday. He was staring right into the eyes of the preacher.

"We must obey the authority God has put over us,"

the preacher said. "We don't need outsiders stirring up seeds of bitterness and discontentment with their murmurings against our brothers."

When the sermon was over, Daddy waited in line to shake the preacher's hand like always. But Sterling went out the side door. Mother gathered with a group of her friends, chatting, while Hattie and I stood around and waited.

Mr. Bagby walked over to Daddy. He didn't notice Hattie and me. I stepped behind a tree to listen.

"Your boy Sterling is certainly growing up," he said.

"That he is. Thinks he's a man," Daddy answered.

"I suspect he'll be going off to school soon," Mr. Bagby replied.

"He hopes to, sir. He's kind of hoping to get that scholarship."

"Couldn't go to a finer family."

"Thank you, sir."

"I've always been able to count on you, Ezra," Mr. Bagby said, moving closer to Daddy and speaking in a low voice. "Things are going to get tough. These guys are going to come after us. We might even be graced by John L. Lewis himself. They're promising the moon to these men. You and I both know they can't deliver. But there are a lot of people who are going to believe them, going to do whatever they say. Keep an eye on that boy of yours. I wouldn't want him to get caught up in this mess."

"I aim to," Daddy answered.

"They're going to lean on you hard 'cause you're a friend of mine, and if they can get your boy to cross over, it'll be a victory. But I want you to know, I appreciate all the work you've done for me over the years."

Daddy shook his head. "Thank you, sir. I've just been doing my job."

"You've always done it well."

"You have a good afternoon, sir," Daddy said as Mr. Bagby walked away.

"Hattie, let's go on home," I said, and we started down the road toward our house.

"What's wrong with you?" she asked.

"You're too little to understand. But there's going to be trouble."

"Did Sterling do something wrong?"

"It looks like Daddy and Sterling are going to be on opposite sides of all this union talk. Daddy thinks that Mr. Bagby is right, that he doesn't have to join the union to work. But Sterling thinks that the union is good and that all the miners should go and join up."

"Who's right?"

"I don't know," I answered.

"I heard that the union men are going to blow up the whole town if the miners don't go on strike!"

"What! Who told you that?" I stopped walking and grabbed her arm.

"Sharon." Hattie's face looked pale.

"Don't worry." I wrapped my arm around her. "No

one will blow up the town." I hoped it was true. "But I wouldn't be surprised if there's fighting."

"Can anyone stop it?"

"All I know is we're going to try to keep Sterling out of trouble."

On Sundays Grandma always fixed a big supper. She didn't go to church with us, said she preferred to commune with God quiet-like in her own way. She wasn't much of a joiner, never joined the Ladies' Auxiliary or went to quilting bees. She always read her Bible on the porch in the morning and could quote Scripture better than the preacher.

When we got home, dinner was on the table: fried potatoes, pork chops, yams, green beans, corn, pickles—all of our favorites. Mother and I were helping Grandma fill the last of the glasses with lemonade.

"Do you think God's on Daddy's side?" I asked.

"What do you mean?" Mother said.

"It seemed that the preacher was saying that union men are bad. Is that true?"

"When it comes to the unions, a lot of people see things differently. May Graham told me that their preacher has been preaching on Moses and deliverance like the union men are heroes."

"Whose side is God on?" I asked.

"God is on all our sides," Mother answered.

"How can that be?" Hattie said.

"God is bigger than the mines or the union or this whole county. That's how."

I was thinking about what Mother had said when Grandma started talking. She was slow to speak, and we listened when she did.

"It's going to happen again," she said. "All the fighting and killing, like when I was a child." Grandma was full of memories that kept her quiet and thinking most of the day. "Your grandpappy was a union man."

"He was?" I was surprised.

Sterling came to the doorway when he heard Grandma.

"My father died in a mine, and I don't want yours to."

"What happened?" Sterling asked.

"When I was a child, the mines were even more hateful than they are now. They'd kill dozens at a time, men with babies and wives, leaving them with nothing. And little children would be down there crawling in the black, digging all day just to eat. No matter how hard men worked, they couldn't seem to get any money saved. The company owned their houses and practically everything in them. Why, my family had to borrow so much from the store that we really didn't own much of anything ourselves. Everyone had to. There was nothing to do but strike, to fight for some way out of that life. The unions came down to help us families. Even Mother Jones came to lend a hand."

"Who is she?" Hattie asked.

"She was a big strong woman, helped with the labor cause. People didn't want to cross her and she knew it. My mother said she was coarse. She was, but she managed to help the men get something from the owners, even spent some time in jail for it. By the time she arrived, we were all living in tents 'cause we'd been thrown out of the company homes. It was cold and damp and we were all sick. Governor Hatfield came all the way from Charleston carrying his doctor bag to treat the sick ones. Came secretly, not wanting the mine owners to know. My baby sister Delila was down with cholera then, but she was too far gone by the time he arrived for a doctor to do any good.

"The Paint Creek mine finally organized and the union helped us for a while. But then my daddy was kilt when one of the mines collapsed. I was seventeen. Your grandpappy was just getting ready to start his shift when it happened. He came to tell me. He was so kind I began to love him then. We got married the next year and moved here.

"There was no union here, but things seemed to be better anyhow, so Grandpappy never joined the union once we left Paint Creek. We tried to farm as much as we could to avoid the mines. But they draw men in, pulling them under with wages in scrip so that they can't live without them again. We were lucky it didn't happen to us."

"Have you ever been back to Paint Creek, Grandma?"

"Once, but the town had dried up. Used to be, people would come from as far away as Cincinnati to do business there. But the union and the machines made them go."

"Union?" Sterling said. "How did the union make them leave?"

"It milked the cow dry, so the farmer had to go somewhere else. After a time, the union bosses started looking an awful lot like the mine owners. And the machines, well, I heard tell that the new machines do the work of ten men. Even John Henry couldn't beat the machine. Died trying."

It was true that something had driven people out of Clay too. Houses sat empty. The laurel and honeysuckle and a host of other vines took over any chance they got and covered a house within a few years of its owner's absence. Fences once fit for keeping goats were broken, beaten down and barely visible in the summer and could no longer hold even a milk cow. There were lots of such places in these hills.

I wondered what Sterling thought of all Grandma had said. Grandma didn't see things like most people, in black and white, right and wrong. She said now, "Good people are living on both sides of the camp."

Chapter 8

Mama and I went to church on Sunday like we always did. But every time I'd try to listen to what the preacher said, I'd see elephants walking in front of me, or a strong man lifting a huge set of weights. I had set my mind on collecting enough pop bottles to go to the circus.

Mama was talking to Mrs. Braxton after the service, so I stood kicking at the dirt, waiting for her to finish.

"What do you want, Clarence?" she asked, annoyed.

"I just wanted to tell you I'm going into Clay."

"What for?"

"To get some pop bottles."

"On a Sunday?"

"The circus is only five days away."

"Don't you want to come home and eat dinner first?"

"I'm not hungry. Just save me a plate."

"Come home and take those good clothes off," she said, and turned back to talk to Mrs. Braxton.

"I promise I won't get them dirty." I ran off down the road.

Clay was an old town with stone homes that had been there as long as my mama could remember. It was big compared to Widon, and most people from the company town went there to get away. The trees grew tall in people's yards and spread their branches wide, perfect for hanging old tires or wooden swings. The Elk River ran right beside the town, and the luckiest people got to back their yard up against it and put in a boat in the summer. They took a chance that the river might overrun its banks in a heavy rain, but to fish every day, it would have been a chance worth taking. Everyone else lived across the road, on the side of the hill or on top of it. The mountains formed a steep pitch, allowing room for only the river, a house and the road before it cut right up the hill.

In Clay people wore hats, not just the women but the men too. People were looser with their money, and I'd have better luck looking for stray pop bottles there than in Widon. Every kid in Widon would have had dibs on the bottles there long ago.

Widow Sommers was my first stop. She wore thick pink powder on her cheeks. Strands of beads hung about her neck and wrist and jingled when she walked in her low-heeled shoes. I figured she might not care about pop bottles the way Mama did. My mama would never have given a bottle away. She saved tags and tokens and trinkets and ticket stubs from everything she ever did. Kept most of them in a drawer by her bedside and put what overflowed in a box under the bed. On rainy days, I'd pull out the box and give it a look. I'd run my fingers over the inlaid flowers, cut from mother of pearl. I'd open it carefully, not wanting to disturb the things inside. There were movie stubs, withered and torn, that said SATURDAY MATINEE; nickel tokens from the fair rides; letters I wouldn't dare read; dried flowers tied around pins, half their petals missing; and photo post-cards of people smiling and ladies wearing floppy hats. I'd pick up a picture of my grandma when she was not much older than me. Her dark hair curled around her face, her skin untouched by wrinkles.

My mama saved bottles too, and jars and tin cans for dried corn for the birds and sometimes for cut flowers. Nothing was wasted. Pop said that she had lived through the Depression and was determined to come out ahead if ever there was another one.

I was standing on the widow's porch thinking about what to say when I heard the shuffling of her house slippers in the hallway.

"Who's out there?" she yelled, fear in her voice. "I said who's out there?"

"It's just me, Clarence Henderson," I answered in the nicest possible voice.

"Well, what do you want, Clarence, going around scaring a body on a Sunday afternoon?"

"I'm trying to get money to go to the circus and was just wondering if you had any pop or milk bottles that I could return."

"Pop bottles, that's what you want?" she said. "Well, come on in here a minute. I might have a couple. I've been known to drink a grape Nehi a time or two." She grabbed her cane and started back down the hall. I followed close behind her.

"I'd return these bottles myself, but I'm just not able on account of my rheumatism. So this is for the circus, is it?" she said.

"Yes ma'am."

"Why, I haven't been to the circus since I was not much older than you," she said. "I used to love the circus. Go right down there," she said, pointing to the cellar door in the corner of her kitchen. "Watch your head," she yelled when I passed under the door frame into a patch of stale, damp air. "Now, you take all them bottles, you hear? And keep all the change."

"Thank you, Mrs. Sommers." I grabbed them up, two in each hand and four more between my ribs and elbows.

"Now, slip those in here," she said, holding out a paper sack. "You come back and visit sometime."

"All right," I told her, not thinking I would anytime soon.

* * *

The aisles of Mr. Sampson's store were covered with sawdust. My first memory was walking barefoot among them with the scents of cut meat and wood shavings mingling in my nostrils. Mr. Sampson kept the meat in the back, the produce up front and everything else in between, including some clothes and shoes and fishing rods. The storefront window changed with the season. The rubber rafts and swimsuits would probably be replaced in a month with slide rules and pencil boxes. You could buy almost anything a body wanted at Mr. Sampson's store, but since Pop was paid in scrip, we didn't shop there much.

"That's eleven bottles at three cents a bottle. I owe you thirty-three cents." I'd be at the circus in no time. The register pinged open and Mr. Sampson pressed the coins into my hand.

"You're Addison Henderson's boy, ain't you? You tell your pop there's a very important meeting this evening and that we're expecting him."

"Yes sir," I said.

As I headed home, I spotted Henry walking the rails.

"Henry!" I hollered, but he didn't seem to hear me. "Henry, I got something to show you."

That brought his head around. I caught up with him and, breathless, opened my palm.

"That ain't but thirty-some cents. The circus costs two dollars," he said.

"I know, but I got all week."

"Why don't you just ask Mrs. Bagby?"

"My pop don't allow me to take no charity."

"Well, I don't know why not. If a person has got money to give, what's wrong with takin' it? She wants to give it away. She don't have nothin' better to do than to spend her money on poor kids like us."

"I ain't poor."

"If you ain't poor, then how come you can't go to the circus?"

I didn't know the answer exactly. Everyone knew Henry was poor, but I didn't think I was, or the Braxtons or lots of folks. Mama said we hit on hard times sometimes, but we weren't poor like Henry.

He looked down at my bow tie. "Why you wearin' that thing?"

"I've been to church. Why don't you ever go?"

"We ain't churchgoin' people," Henry said. I had never heard a person admit that. It was like saying you wanted to go to hell.

"Why?"

"Don't got no clothes, I guess. I've been thinkin' 'bout gettin' me another dog," he said, changing the subject. "My cousins' coonhound had a litter."

"I thought you already had a dog."

"Old Suzy? She ain't good for much anymore on account of her leg. She got it caught in a trap up over the mountain. She was up there for days before anyone found her. I figured she done runned away."

I would have thought that too. Henry's dog, Suzy, was afraid of most people 'cause she got a kick if she got in anyone's way.

"I wish I could get a dog," I said.

"Why don't you?"

"Pop says they eat too much and get into the chickens."

"That's the good thing about Suzy. We hardly had to feed her nothin', 'cause she got her own food in people's trash and eatin' squirrels. But she's not too good at catchin' squirrels anymore. She's gettin' awful skinny." Henry turned and walked back toward town, not saying goodbye.

I took the tracks most of the way home to avoid the road and the people along it. But when I neared the cutaway to my house, I saw Elizabeth walking by herself in the other direction. I was embarrassed to see her, so I kept quiet. Her eyes stayed fixed on each railroad tie while she mumbled words too soft for me to hear, like some kind of magic spell. She grabbed her chest when she saw me.

"Why, Clarence Henderson, you scared me to death. How long have you been standing there?"

"I haven't been standing here. I've been walking since Bagby Field."

"Well, you shouldn't go sneaking up on people like that," she said.

"I wasn't sneaking up on anybody. I was out collecting pop bottles so I could raise money for the circus."

"Did you get any?"

"Thirty-three cents from Widow Sommers, but I asked everyone else and that was it."

"I wish I could go to the circus too. I've never been." She stepped up along the edge of the track, threw her arms out to the sides like a cross and began carefully moving one foot in front of the other.

"I bet you I can walk further than you, Clarence," she said.

"But I can walk faster." I stepped up on the railing.

"See that old stump right there? The first person that gets to that without falling off wins," she declared. I ran as fast as I could, taking big risky steps along the tracks. I'd almost made it when my body tumbled to the left ahead of my feet. Elizabeth was a good twenty feet back but moving as carefully as a tightrope walker.

"Clarence, don't you remember that story 'bout the tortoise and the hare?" she giggled, and walked slowly past where I'd fallen. "You are fast, though."

Just then we heard a loud shriek coming from the canopy of trees right over our heads.

"What was that?" she cried.

"I don't know. I've never heard anything like that before."

I started toward the trees.

"Don't go over there, Clarence! Whatever it is might eat you or something."

I laughed. "It's just some kind of animal."

"Maybe it's a bobcat that's rabid."

"I'll be careful." I got a bit closer and we saw something flashing like the lights from a camera.

"Clarence!" Elizabeth yelled.

Whatever it was was too high in the trees to see clearly. But we traced the flicker of light as the ripples through the leaves finally disappeared over the hill.

"Clarence, seeing that you're going the same direction I am, would you mind if I walked along with you?"

"I guess not." I smiled a bit.

"You think it's funny that I'm so scared, but you never know what kind of animal might be around here."

"I wasn't smiling at that." I was thinking how I never thought a girl would ask to walk with me.

Chapter 9

"Mother, are we going to go to the circus this year? You promised we'd get to go sometime," Hattie asked.

"I wish I could tell you yes, but Daddy might have to stop working if the miners strike."

"He'd better stop working, otherwise he'll be a scab." Sterling didn't look at Mother.

"May the Lord have mercy on you if your father hears you talk that way. He is a God-fearing man who has honest differences with the union men, differences you don't know enough to understand," Mother said.

"I heard talk that there were two hundred union men coming down from Pittsburgh, and some from Logan," Sterling said.

Mother held the towel still in her hands and stopped drying the pots.

"Where do you hear such things?" she said, looking at him like she'd never seen him before.

"I just heard it," he answered. "I'm going for a walk."

"Sterling Braxton, you best steer clear of any union talk or you'll bring shame on your daddy. You take Elizabeth along with you."

"I don't want to take her with me!"

"Why not?" Mother asked.

Sterling's eyes stayed fixed on the floorboards, his face tight with anger.

"I'll get my shoes," I said.

Mother touched my shoulder as if to tell me to keep an eye on Sterling. But I didn't turn my head. Sterling and I had always had a pact between us. We didn't tell on one another and we kept each other's secrets. He had kept most of his to himself lately.

Sterling had put a good distance between us along the road. I was out of breath when I reached him.

"Where are we going?"

"I don't know where you're going, but I'm going to a union meeting in town."

"Mother just told you to stay away from them!"

"She doesn't understand."

"She knows more than you think."

"Do you think Pop is going to know what's best for the future of the mines? He's always the last to do anything. We don't even have a telephone."

"Daddy says they're no good."

"What do *you* think? Stop spouting what he says."

"I guess I really don't know. Maybe I should come with you tonight just to see what it's all about."

"Tony Polita is going to tell us all the unionizing plan."

"Who's Tony Polita?"

"He's a miner who works for John L. Lewis."

"Are you sure he doesn't work for the communists?"

"You've been listening to Daddy too long."

"I was joking," I said. "But I would like to know about it all. Maybe Mother won't get mad if I'm there to keep an eye on you."

"Well, maybe you'll be the first girl in Clay to join the union!"

Sterling and I laughed. When we got to town, there were men outside the school gym talking, waiting for the meeting to start. They were mostly my father's age except for a couple of Sterling's friends. I didn't see any women or girls. As the men started to file inside, I spotted Johnny Beasley in the back with a couple other boys from school. I stood watching him, frozen for a moment, until Sterling pushed me forward.

"You know my sister, don't you, Johnny," Sterling said with a smirk. I could have kicked him.

"I've seen her around." He smiled at me.

My heart leapt and I opened my mouth to talk, but Sterling rushed us in before I could say hello.

The room was crowded, and I had to stand close between Johnny and Sterling along the back wall as Mr. Sampson called for everyone's attention. I looked straight ahead, but from the corner of my eye, I noticed Johnny glancing at me.

I pretended not to see him, but I worried he might notice that my face was red with excitement. This was how I felt when I had to stand in front of the class to read a poem I'd written.

Mr. Sampson stepped up on a milk crate to speak into a small microphone. "I want to thank you all for coming. It's exciting to see such a great turnout here in the last nonunion county in West Virginia." The men cheered loudly.

"They say this place is backward, but when I see so many men wanting to be a part of the United Mine Workers, I know they're wrong. You men understand that our future depends on being a part of the UMW." Johnny and Sterling hooted and pounded their hands together along with the rest of the men. Johnny put his fingers to his lips and whistled.

"Now here's someone who can tell you why we need to convince our neighbors and friends to stick to-gether to bring Mr. Bagby to the bargaining table. Gentlemen, Mr. Tony Polita."

There were more cheers and clapping. And then one of the handsomest men I ever saw stepped up on the box. He looked like a movie star.

"It's a little warm in here," he said, taking off his jacket and rolling up his sleeves to reveal his strong arms.

"I want you gentlemen to know, I'm not just some

outsider that doesn't understand your struggles. I was a miner, my father was a miner and I understand who you are. I am coming to give you a voice, to help lift your families up to the level of the rest of the country. What I need from you is your solidarity. We all have to agree to a walkout in a few weeks. We're going to rid West Virginia of the last vestige of bloodsucking mine owners."

After the cheering stopped, Tony began again. "We're going to secure pensions for every miner working, so that if he gets hurt or is too old to work, his family doesn't have to suffer. His loved ones will know that the UMW will stand beside them and see that they're taken care of."

I couldn't imagine why Daddy wouldn't want that. Mr. Polita seemed like a good man, at least no different from any of the miners I knew.

Sterling listened as if he was committing Tony's speech to memory. I looked over at Johnny Beasley and he was looking right at me. I turned around quick but felt my cheeks go red again. I tried to concentrate on what Tony was saying.

"This sounds pretty good, doesn't it?" Johnny nudged me.

I nodded, feeling the rush of my heart when he looked at me.

After the meeting was over, Sterling and I walked outside with Johnny.

"I can't wait for the walkout," Sterling said.

"Polita sure got you riled up," Johnny said.

"Do you think they'll hurt anybody?" I asked.

"Only people fool enough to get in their way," Johnny said.

But what would happen to Daddy? "Couldn't the union men just go and talk to Mr. Bagby and try to work out something before all the fighting started?" Johnny and Sterling laughed outright.

"Mr. Bagby isn't going to do anything he doesn't have to. But this time he has to comply with our demands."

"Or what?"

"Or what?" Johnny and Sterling said in unison, mocking me. "That's what's going to make this strike so exciting," Johnny added. He stopped short where the road took a turn and looked at us. "Don't take any wooden nickels." He winked.

I smiled.

Sterling and I picked up our pace as the sky darkened.

"So what did you think?" he asked.

"Mr. Polita talked like he really was coming to help do good."

"Now do you understand why I want the UMW?"

"The trouble is, now I don't understand why Daddy doesn't. What are you going to say to Mother and Daddy?" I said.

"I ain't afraid of the truth."

* * *

When we walked in the door, Daddy said, "Where have you children been?"

"At the union meeting in town," Sterling answered.

"You too, Elizabeth?" Mother asked.

"I thought I should stay with Sterling. They didn't do anything bad there. They didn't talk about killing people or blowing up bridges or anything like that."

"Of course they don't talk about blowing up bridges. They're trying to pull in people that are fool enough to believe their promises of a better everything," Daddy said.

"You had no business going there, Elizabeth." Mother went to pull the curtains.

"But I want to understand what all this strike talk is about."

"That's no place for a girl."

"Things will be better if you join them." Sterling tried to deliver Mr. Polita's lines like they were his own.

"If you join the unions you have to do what the UMW bosses tell you," Daddy said. "I think for myself. I don't like someone telling me when I can and cannot work. I have a right to work when my family needs food. Randall Bagby has put food on my table for years and I can't complain about that."

"What about Ollie Hensley?" Sterling asked. "You said yourself he's as crooked as a dog's leg, always cuddling up to the inspectors."

The whole town knew about Mr. Hensley. He was the foreman at the mine and seemed to always work Daddy's shift. When he was working, the men were never sure if the scales were right, if they were getting paid for their work. The mine inspectors were all appointed by the politicians and would likely pass any mine, no matter how bad it was, if the foreman gave them something. Mr. Hensley always did—a free dinner, nice cigars. Folks said he had a whole box of cigars from Cuba in his desk just in case the inspector stopped by.

"There are bad apples in every business. I bet there'll be crooked men in the union too," Daddy replied.

"But why doesn't Mr. Bagby fire Mr. Hensley?" I asked.

"Because Mr. Hensley makes money for Mr. Bagby. He's a businessman."

"If the unions were here, we could get rid of men like Mr. Hensley."

"I don't know about that, son."

"But we'd have some way to talk to the owners and negotiate for better things," Sterling said.

"Mr. Bagby pays me more than the union men get paid anyhow. And mining is the best-paying job in this county. You know I tried selling cars and working at the store, but I always came back to Mr. Bagby and he always gave me back my job."

"Why did you leave it if it paid so well?" I asked.

"It's killing work. No one really wants to be a miner. But around here, for someone like me who doesn't have much education, you can't beat the pay."

"What about all the mine accidents?" Sterling said. "The UMW will get better safety standards so there won't be as many accidents, and if something happens, they take care of you until you get back to work. And if you get killed, then there's a pension for Mother."

"Son, nothing is free. All those benefits cost money. That's what the communists said in Russia. 'Stick together, things will get better.' And things did get better—for those in charge. Everybody else lost their freedom."

"The UMW isn't communist," Sterling said.

"They may not be, but why give them the power to make your decisions?"

"Because together we can have more power than we do by ourselves." Sterling folded his arms.

"I'll tell you who'll have power—the union bosses, not you." Daddy leaned toward Sterling, his face red. "This family will not be a part of the UMW."

"That's 'cause this family is scabs." Sterling pushed himself from the table.

Mother put her fork down and looked right at me.

Our dinner table was just like the town. It had divided like the Red Sea.

Chapter 10

We didn't see too much of Pop. He was working with the UMW just outside Widon, setting up a mess and some tents for them. The threat of a strike hung heavy in the air.

For me, the storm had already begun with their stares. Whenever someone new moved to town, they'd gawk at me—especially the little ones, pointing fingers and whispering to their mothers, who usually hushed them proper before they looked themselves. Then they'd smile. The miners almost always looked over my head to avoid me. They wouldn't say anything at all, not "Howdy" or "It's a nice day, isn't it." Just a look like I was deaf and mute too.

"We better load up the truck, Clarence," Mama said.

"What for?"

"We best fill our cupboards while we have the chance. Get that scrip out of the jar."

"Are the strikers going to steal the food?"

"No, but they might block the tracks and keep food from coming in."

"Most of the strikers live in Widon. Why would they block a train that would help them?" Pop said. "That doesn't make any sense."

"I've never known strikers to make much sense," Mama answered. "Get in the truck, Clarence."

I wanted to drive. Pop had let me a couple of times, but Mama said no. When Mama worried about one thing, her worry spilled over into everything else.

I waited outside the company store while she went in. Pop kept some money in a bank in Clay, but we kept scrip in a jar in the kitchen. The fifty dollars of scrip Mama had would only buy a little more than half of what real money would buy at Mr. Sampson's store in Clay. But for most folks, Clay was too far to travel for groceries.

Next to the grocer's was a platform for loading and unloading the train. There were union men coming in carrying packs on their backs, fixing to set up camp. Some looked like regular old miners; others wore hats and carried guns careless-like over their shoulders. Henry was there too. It was the most interesting place to be, so I wasn't surprised to see him. I knew he would be a union man; something about the way he'd been holding his head lately told me that.

"Hey, Henry," I said, walking toward him. He just looked at me and spat.

"Are you going to the circus tomorrow?" he asked.

I looked down. I'd searched for bottles all week, got up early and stayed out late. But I only had a little more than a dollar to show for it.

"You didn't get a ticket, did you? I knew you wouldn't, fool. Who would give you bottles anyway?"

I turned to walk away.

"I'll tell you all about it tomorrow," he yelled at my back.

"I don't want to hear." I stood against the wall of the store, rolling the coins around in my pocket, watching the men get off the train.

Henry grabbed one of the men's bags and carried it to a truck. A colored man got off next. I stared at him for a while and studied his dark eyes and face. There were some coloreds who lived on the other side of Widon. We went to school with some of them, but I didn't really know them. They had their own churches, restaurants and dances, and it seemed they preferred it that way or at least a lot of other people did. This man came off the platform, followed by a group of white miners. He smiled like he was one of them, but I knew he wasn't. Chances were, he'd been picked on, called names, maybe even beat up. He stared right at me as he passed, looking at me like he knew me, like he knew all about me. Mama came out just then and I stood up to meet her, avoiding his stare.

"Carry these boxes for me now, Clarence," she said.

Chapter 11

When the circus rolled into town that Friday morning, most of the kids in Clay were there. Hattie and I walked the whole way to town to see it.

A crowd of kids gathered around the back of the tents watching. Henry Fulton and his brothers and sisters lined up to direct the others. They claimed that the circus was old hat to them, since they had been every year, courtesy of the Bagbys.

"Watch out, now. The elephants will be coming thataway. See that man with the gold hair?" Henry hollered, pointing to a man with great big muscles like Tarzan's and hair the color of straw. "He wears a leopard skin underneath his clothes and tames the lions." The lions' cages ran together like the cars of a train. They sat empty, the doors that separated them raised and no lions in sight.

"Maybe they escaped," Hattie said.

"I wonder," I answered. The cages were small, with bars like a prison, and I kind of hoped they *had* escaped.

"Before the circus, you can pay fifty cents and go in there." Henry pointed to a small red-and-white striped tent. "That's where they keep the freaks of nature, like the snake lady. Hey, Clarence, if you join the freak show, they'd let you in the big top for free. You could forget all about the pop bottles."

I turned around to see Clarence. He stood alone against the bars of one of the cages, his face to the ground, hidden from view. The top of his head shimmered in the sunlight. He looked nothing like a freak.

I turned back to see a chimpanzee sitting on the lion tamer's back. He screeched and showed his teeth as they walked past the crowd. Henry's little sister crawled onto his shoulders for a better view.

A short, stocky man with a large green dragon tattoo on his arm ordered people around. His skin was weathered and his hair oily. Under one arm he kept a rolled-up newspaper, and he carried a dome-topped cage with a small monkey inside, the kind that usually sat atop a barrel organ. The monkey hopped around the cage, screeching and showing its teeth to the crowd.

There wasn't much that separated the kids that got to go and the ones that didn't—maybe a good crop, a daddy who didn't drink, one less child, a generous grandmother or an older son's wages. Grandma Braxton's rheumatism kept us from going this year because Daddy had to pay for her medicine. Grandma protested, but none of us wanted to see her in pain.

"Wouldn't it be nice, Elizabeth," Hattie asked dreamily, "if we could meet one of those lady trapeze artists? I want to grow up and look glamorous like her someday," she said, looking at the tall, dark women with big black eyes.

The circus women looked different from any other women I'd seen, covered with streaks of red and blue and black on their eyes and lips.

"Me and Dara Nicely have been practicing our handstands," Hattie said.

"I'm going to be a writer," I said. I'd meant to keep it a secret until I had completed my first novel, but it just sort of slipped out. I thought that everyone near me might stop and turn around, surprised. But Sterling and Hattie heard nothing but circus sounds. It didn't matter. I had set my dream free, loosed it from its secret spot. Saying a dream aloud was like adding oil to a squeaky wheel. The covers of my favorite books passed before my eyes, and I almost forgot the circus until one of the monkeys started screeching.

"What happened?" I said to Hattie.

"Didn't you see?" she said, her toes curled to raise her a few inches above the head in front of her. "That monkey just bit that man."

The man picked up a strap and laid it across the

monkey's back until it curled its lip and showed its teeth. I covered my eyes. "Ooh, poor monkey!"

"Oh, it's probably all part of the show. You'll see if you come with me tomorrow."

John Beasley stood so close that I felt my breath go short. The circus with Johnny! What should I say?

"How did you like the meeting the other night, Elizabeth?" he said.

"It was very interesting. I'm glad I went," I said. "There was a lot said I hadn't heard before."

"Why did you come?"

"I wanted to know more. Besides, Mother wanted me to keep Sterling out of trouble."

"I suppose you're good at that, keeping him out of trouble."

"He's good at getting in it, I know that."

"Weren't you afraid to go there, being the only girl?"

"Why should I be afraid?"

"I just don't know too many girls who would have been interested in going to a union meeting."

"Maybe they just never get the chance."

"I'd like to take you to something even more exciting. We'll go inside the tents, of course." He ran his fingers through his hair, coal-black like his eyes. He was wearing a T-shirt with his number on it, 56. I knew the number 'cause I'd watched him play so many games.

"Well, what about it?" he asked again.

"Well, I would be delighted, John Beasley." It sounded so silly, *delighted*, like I was an old woman. Could he tell I'd never been on a date before?

"I'll come by your house around six o'clock," he said.

"Okay," I said, smiling. Blood was rushing to my head. Johnny walked away, pretending not to notice.

I covered my neck, crossed my fingers. Mother had to say yes.

Chapter 12

The circus was like a dream. Johnny and I sat in the middle of the front row breathing in the smells of animals and sawdust. I couldn't keep my head still. There was too much to see. I didn't want to miss a thing, except the tightrope walker, who I almost couldn't bear watching. He stumbled a bit, tilted his big balancing stick to the right and then the left. The crowd swooned and swayed along with him, and I shut my eyes until I heard applause. Johnny laughed so much he spilled his popcorn when an elephant walked right beside me. I just kept thinking of Hattie and how she would have died to sit next to a real elephant. I knew why Clarence had wanted to come so badly. It was worth all the pop bottles he'd collect in a whole year.

I couldn't decide if my head was spinning from the circus or from being with John Beasley and sharing the pink cotton candy and popcorn and soda pop. He had bought them all, said his father had given him two dollars to buy anything he wanted. Johnny's dad was one of the richest people in Clay, next to Mr. Bagby, of course. He sold equipment to the mines and had lived here all his life. They lived in a real pretty old stone house right downtown. Sterling said they even had a pool table in the basement.

At the circus, lots of people that I didn't even know knew my name said "Hello, Elizabeth." Sally and her parents sat a couple rows behind us. When I turned to look into the crowd, I saw her staring at us. I acted like I didn't see her watching. I had to smile and sit up taller with everyone looking at me. I'd ironed the crease in my church dress twice so it wouldn't be so obvious that the hem had been let down. Johnny made me feel pretty, even if my dress wasn't. He smiled at me each time a performer shone, eager to see my reaction.

He took me right home after the circus since it was already way past dark by the time it was over. Johnny had his own red truck, a Chevy that was a gift from his father for his sixteenth birthday. Sterling longed to have his own car too. He drew pictures of cars and pasted the cutouts from soap boxes along the walls of his room. I couldn't help thinking of him when we careened around every turn until the dust blew like ribbons from the tires.

"Why are you going so fast?" I asked.

" 'Cause I like to, don't you? I didn't think you

would be afraid of anything. A girl that can go to a union meeting ought not to be afraid to drive a little fast."

"Not this fast!" I clutched the seat with all my might, feeling the night air whip against my cheeks. I looked over to see Johnny, his face entranced by the headlights of his truck. He didn't dare turn his eyes away from the road. Just as we rounded the mountain, we saw a train, its headlight pulsing through the trunks of the trees. Johnny sped up, racing the train to the crossing half a mile down the hill.

"Stop!

"Yeehaw!" he yelled, speeding just ahead of the engine. "We're going to beat this baby!"

"Don't!" I screamed.

He grinned, his fingers tight around the steering wheel.

We sped past the crossing with the train's whistle at our backs.

My heart was racing so I could barely speak. When I caught my breath, I looked at him, his face still holding that wide smile.

"Why did you do that!"

"What's the matter?" he said. "Don't you trust me?"

"We could have been killed." I was trembling as he looked at me with eyes like liquid ink. How handsome he was!

My whole family stood against the porch railing

like they were waiting for news from a fire. My eyes sank in embarrassment. Daddy wasted no time coming up to the car. I put my hand on the handle to get out.

"You're driving awfully fast, son."

"We were just having a little fun," Johnny replied.

"You take it easier next time, you hear?" Daddy said.

"Yes sir." He didn't get out of the car, just waved goodbye when I stepped up on the porch. He drove off and I watched his taillights disappear into the darkness.

Just as Mother was closing the screen door, a wild screaming came from up the road. I might have thought it was an animal if the voice hadn't been screaming Daddy's name.

"Ezra, Ezra!"

Daddy and Sterling raced down the porch steps. When the screaming got closer, I could see it was one of Daddy's miner friends, Mr. Murphy, with a big rope around his neck.

"They've killed them, every one of them!" screamed Mr. Murphy.

"What are you talking about?" Daddy asked.

"They shot all of them miners going to work the number four. They were going to hang me but I ran away."

"Who shot them?" Daddy lifted the noose off Mr. Murphy's neck and put his arm across the man's shoulders.

"The union men! Nobody I knew. Must have been those men sent to organize."

"Sterling, get my gun, and run over and tell Addie Henderson to get the sheriff."

Sterling kept staring at the noose Daddy held in his hands.

"Don't just stand there—go, boy!"

Sterling raced back to the house.

My stomach went sick. I kept thinking of those men at the meeting, Tony Polita and Mr. Sampson. I couldn't imagine them shooting anyone dead.

Daddy and Mr. Murphy ran up the road in the dark with the gun.

"Won't you wait for the sheriff?" Mother yelled.

"No time to waste. I don't want anyone else to be killed."

"Then why are you taking that gun?" Grandma hollered. Daddy kept running while the rest of us went inside to wait.

"Why?" I asked, shaking. "Why would they put that rope around his neck?"

"They aimed to lynch him or scare him to death," Grandma answered.

"The strike hasn't even started and those union men are already killing." Mother's anger showed itself as she whisked the broom heartily in each corner of the room.

Grandma prayed and I closed my eyes. I kept thinking of Mr. Murphy, his face twisted in terror. He was usually so calm, so steady. Then I thought of Johnny moments before, smiling at me, neither one of us thinking a thing about the unions or the miners or anything but having fun. Sterling had about convinced me that we needed unions, but if this was the way they operated, I understood why Daddy wanted nothing to do with them.

It wasn't long before we heard someone kicking up the gravel outside.

Sterling burst through the door, smiling.

"Why are you laughing, Sterling Braxton? Don't you know men died tonight?" Mother screamed.

"No one died. Addie Henderson said it was all a joke, just meant to scare those guys. There weren't no shooting, only dynamite. It was just a warning, to let them know what might happen if they work during the strike."

"What kind of people scare a man half to death with a noose?" I asked. "How can you render a smile at that?"

"Go up the road and find your daddy. And don't let him see you smiling," Mother said.

Chapter 13

With all the commotion, Hattie forgot to ask me about the circus. I closed my eyes, remembering each moment. When we had first arrived, Johnny had taken my hand and led me into the tent. I'd never held anyone's hand before and I had been surprised by its softness. I'd held it loosely. I'd felt his breath against my shoulder when he whispered something about the clowns in my ear. I'd scooted closer to him, hoping he would whisper again.

It was hard to sleep. I kept wishing I could see him, see his eyes look at me brightly like they did when we were driving. I had never had so much fun in all my life. It wasn't just being at the circus; it was being alone in a car with him. It made me feel older, freer. Had he had as much fun as I had?

In the dark, my smile faded. Had he seen Mr. Murphy running up the road?

Scaring Mr. Murphy would make men like Daddy more determined to resist the union. I didn't blame him. I'd heard stories about coloreds being lynched, the horrors done in the dark of night by men afraid to let their faces be seen. Were union men as evil as they were?

At lunch the next day, Daddy said, "Son, if those are the kind of men you want to be around, I'm ashamed of you." Sterling walked out onto the porch to sit and stew. Hattie and I followed, and she started up with a rhyme she'd heard from a miner's daughter.

"Jenny wink, Jenny wink, where've you been?
Blowing up bridges and I'll do it again.
Jenny wink, Jenny wink, what'd you do?
Shoot me a man and I'll shoot you too."

"Oh, shut up with that stupid song," Sterling snapped. "You don't even know what you're singing about."

"You don't think it was right what they did to Mr. Murphy, do you?" I asked.

"I'm not saying it was right, but I understand why they did it. Sometimes you have to do things like that to get people's attention. No one got hurt."

"What if the union people are just a bunch of thugs and troublemakers?"

"They're not. They may not always do everything

80

right, but I know things will be better if we unionize. Things have got to get better than they are now."

"I never knew you to be starving."

"We're not starving, but we don't have nothin' either."

The screen door creaked open and Mother handed me a jar of jelly.

"Take this over to Sally's house, would you?"

Sally's mom said that Mother's was the best blackberry jelly she'd tasted, so Mother made a point of sending her some when she made it.

I could use a walk. Sally was peeling potatoes at the kitchen table when I stepped up on the front porch. She worked intently, her large brown eyes fixed on her hands. I noticed how much she looked like her mother. "Elizabeth!" she cried.

"My mother sent this over to y'all," I said, and set the jar on the counter.

"Come sit and tell me all about last night."

I pulled up a chair beside her and watched her knife move quickly over the potatoes. "You were there. Wasn't it wonderful? Especially the elephants."

"I'm not talking about the circus, I'm talking about Johnny. What was that like?"

"Oh, I don't know. It was fun."

"Fun! Tell me more! Did he drive you home?"

"Yes, but he started racing the train and made Daddy mad."

"Did you like him?"

"I liked him. He bought me all kinds of candy and

popcorn. And he talked to me the whole time. I never knew a boy could talk so much."

"I saw you sitting awfully close."

"Not that close!"

"Are you going to see him again?"

"I'll see him again at school."

"Are you going to go out with him again?"

"I don't know. It was only last night."

"Would you go if he asked you?"

"I suppose."

She stopped peeling a minute and leaned back in her chair. "Elizabeth Braxton and Johnny Beasley. Who'd have thought it?"

"What's that supposed to mean?"

"Oh, nothing, just that—it's just surprising, that's all. You know, you—you're . . ." she stammered, "well, and Johnny is the most popular boy in school. I don't think anyone expected he would be dating you. It's not that Angela and I aren't happy for you. It's just so amazing."

"It isn't like we're going steady or anything."

"I know, I know. I just can't wait to see what happens."

I walked home thinking. I knew I wasn't the most popular girl in school, but Sally acted like I wasn't good enough for Johnny or something.

I hadn't been home from Sally's ten minutes when I saw his red truck coming up our road, blowing up dust behind him. Sterling and I were sitting on the porch, clear of the heat of the afternoon sun. I hadn't expected him so soon. I tried to smooth my hair. I bit my lips and pinched my cheeks just as Sterling turned to see me.

"Getting all pretty for your boyfriend?"

"Be quiet."

I sat on the porch like nothing was on my mind, waiting for Johnny to get out of the truck. He stuck his head out and waved to Sterling.

"What are you doing out here?" Sterling asked.

"I don't know. I wanted to see if Elizabeth might want to walk a ways."

I smiled at him and turned to open the screen door. "Mother, Johnny Beasley is here. He wants to know if I could walk a little while."

She looked at me with a knowing eye that made me turn away. "Don't be gone long."

"I won't."

When I went outside, Johnny was waiting with his hands in his pockets, watching Sterling take his jackknife to a piece of wood. "What are you making?" Johnny asked.

"I'm not sure yet. Maybe a turkey call."

I turned to Johnny. "Where do you want to go?"

"How 'bout up the old mine road?"

"Okay."

Once we got out of sight of the house, Johnny reached down to grab my hand.

"Thanks for taking me to the circus. It was one of the best times I've ever had."

"I had a lot of fun too," he said. We walked along in silence while I tried to think of something to say.

"Do you walk on this road much?" he asked.

"I come out here all the time."

"What for?"

"I just like to walk."

"By yourself?"

"Sometimes Sterling comes with me. But I like to go by myself most of the time."

"Why?"

"Just to be alone, to think and all."

"I'd rather have someone to talk to."

It was true. I had hardly ever seen Johnny Beasley by himself. He was usually with the other football players.

Since it was spring, the woods were full of animals stirring, mostly squirrels and birds rustling around in the leaves and briars. It took us a few minutes to realize that something bigger was out there, hidden in the dense mountain laurel on the hill below us. Johnny pulled my hand back and put his finger over his mouth to hush me. Hearing the crackling leaves, I tightened my fingers around his. "What do you think it is?"

"Probably just a deer."

We moved to the edge of the road, aware of each sound. "Clarence Henderson and I heard the strangest noise the other day coming home from town," I whispered.

"What were you doing with Clarence Henderson?"

"Just walking."

"He's strange," Johnny said.

"People are mean to him. He's not so bad."

"Oh, don't feel sorry for him. If he didn't act so weird, people wouldn't tease him."

I wished I hadn't told him about Clarence. Sally and Angela would never have walked with Clarence. "I wasn't really walking with him. I was by myself and he kind of came up behind me. We were racing on the rails when we heard this terrible shriek. It was kind of like a scream, but none I'd ever heard before."

He squeezed my hand and pulled me to him. His lips pressed hard against mine and I felt his skin rough against my cheek. It wasn't the soft kiss I had imagined my first would be. My arms wrapped around him and I felt the dampness on the back of his shirt from the heat. He stepped back and we kept walking down the road. I stared at his feet, too embarassed to look him in the eye, until he stopped short.

"I think I see someone hiding behind that bush down there," he said, squinting toward the creek bed.

"Maybe it's what we heard the other day."

"An animal doesn't wear a white shirt."

"Where?"

"Right there." Johnny pointed over the hill. I glimpsed something white amid the green.

"Who is that?" Johnny said, low and deep.

The white figure scurried across the creek and up the other side until it was lost in the trees.

Had someone seen Johnny kiss me? I wanted to keep it all to myself. I tightened my fingers around his, half afraid and half longing for more of him. The road was as familiar as the walls of my bedroom. I'd never before been afraid to walk it alone. But seeing that stranger in the woods changed something. I'd known the fear of Daddy not coming home from the mine, and of disease. But this fear was stronger. Its grip held my whole family. It turned my world, my secret place, my home into something unknown. I didn't know whether it was the fear of strangers or the talk of violence or the fighting in my own family. Whatever it was, it cast a shadow of doubt and worry even in those places I felt most comfortable. I sensed Johnny felt it too. He was quiet.

"Probably just some kid," he muttered.

"I don't know. With all the talk of a strike, maybe it was someone else. Let's go on back now. Mother told me not to be gone long."

"I won't let anything happen to you, Elizabeth." He dropped my hand to pick up a stick and swing at some of the branches that hung over the road.

My hand felt suddenly cold without his.

"Do you want to go to the spring dance with me?"

"Oh, that would be nice," I said. "I'll have to ask Mother." The dance. I had never imagined I would ever go to a dance, even after Johnny asked me to the circus. I never dared think beyond that night. What would Sally say now? It took my breath just thinking about it.

Before we got too close to the house, he turned to kiss me on the cheek. I wanted to put my arms around him and kiss him again. But he turned and walked off to his truck.

Chapter 14

I hid away that afternoon near the house, clear of Hattie. I wanted to think about Johnny and my first kiss and how he'd held his hand tight around mine when he knew I was afraid. I wanted to think about his deep black eyes and the way he made me feel like someone worth holding, with hair worth stroking. I wanted to think about the dance and what it would be like, what I would wear, what I would say. But there was a grayness hovering over my bright thoughts.

Before the unions, I couldn't have imagined something powerful enough to drive a wedge between my father and brother. I made up my mind to talk to Daddy about it.

I went to bed and waited for everyone else to fall asleep. As I waited, I thought about Johnny. I couldn't remember the feel of his kiss. I shut my eyes tight, hoping it would come back to me, but all I could remember was the smell of his face, splashed with some kind of aftershave. I chuckled at the thought of him putting that on to impress me when I didn't even like the smell of perfume. I almost drifted to sleep but roused myself when I heard Mother shut her bedroom door. I wrapped a robe around my shoulders and walked into the living room to find Daddy puffing on a pipe.

"I want to ask you about something. I don't understand how you and Sterling come to be on different sides about the union."

"I know it must be hard to understand," he said. "Long ago, unions did a lot of good."

"Why don't you like the union?"

"The UMW promises pensions and a host of things, but everything comes at a cost. They'll have to pay dues. Mr. Bagby won't be able to keep on as many men, so some of them will lose their jobs. I don't begrudge a man for fighting if he thinks he's being treated unfairly. But the union makes squeaky wheels out of men, turning them into people who do nothing but complain. I've lived long enough to know that there are some people who aren't going to be happy with anything. The union makes men think they can't change anything without them. I know men have more power together, but I don't want to stand with a bunch of thugs."

"But what if Sterling is right? What if they really

can make things better for all the miners? Wouldn't it be worth joining them?"

"A man has to decide how much he can take. My life working at Bagby's mine is all I expect it to be. There are risks, but I knew that when I took the job. Sterling has to decide how much he can take. I can't decide that for him. But I do know that I don't want to be forced to break my word for someone to hear me. Mr. Bagby is a gentleman, and I aim to treat him as such and have him treat me the same way."

"Does Mr. Bagby always keep his word?"

"Mr. Bagby is a businessman. He makes the decisions that he believes are best for his business. I don't blame him for that. All men make bad decisions. But I think talking to him without the union is better. We got a board of grievances. We meet every six months to discuss things. Sometimes they change. Sometimes they don't."

"Sterling believes that the union is going to make every problem go away," I said.

"In trying to fix things, they're going to make a bunch more problems for themselves and everyone else. But don't be angry with your brother 'cause he thinks differently. He'll figure it out in time and learn to make his own way. So will you one day. I'm proud of you for thinking about such things. You have a fine head on your shoulders and you should trust your own judgment. Don't get caught up in all the talk."

I put my arms around him. "Thanks," I said. "Good night, Daddy."

Somehow I felt that when I laid my head down, I had a better understanding. I could see how Daddy could bear a heavier yoke than Sterling. Sterling wasn't willing to wait for things to get better. He had set his mind to change things no matter what the cost. He had always been that way; even as a kid he'd burn himself drinking hot chocolate before it cooled.

Chapter 15

I stood behind the tree while he kissed her. I ran over the side of the hill as soon as I saw them. I think they spotted me. I hadn't really thought about girls before, but when I saw John Beasley kissing Elizabeth, something in my stomach went sour and I couldn't catch my breath.

When I got to the bottom of the hill, I saw that flash again, just like I'd seen with Elizabeth. It was high in the trees like before, and something called out like a mountain lion stuck in a tree. The sun's rays bounced off of something shiny. I picked up a rock and hurled it into the trees to try to scare the thing out.

Elmer Atkinson swore he'd seen a black panther last fall. Nothing in the woods ever frightened me, not even the sight of a bear. But this sound was strange and unfamiliar, almost spooky. It called out again, a high-pitched *hee-hee* like a laugh. Its silhouette against the bright sky was the size of a raccoon. I crept closer, gently, so as not to crunch the leaves.

I grabbed a tree limb and pulled myself up. When I did, the thing came toward me, crawling on all fours like a possum. But it had a curly tail. I blinked. I could hardly believe my eyes—a real live monkey was in Clay County.

I figured it must have escaped from the circus. "Here, boy," I called. It looked like it was trying to answer me. It came close enough and then stopped and sat up on a limb a stone's throw away. In its hand was my broken looking glass. That's what was flashing at me.

"Here, boy. I won't hurt you." It jumped up and screeched when I edged near it. I thought about going home and getting some food to lure it down, but I didn't want to let it out of my sight. It seemed to be studying me. I watched it until it was time for me to go.

"Goodbye, monkey," I said. "I'll come back tomorrow."

"Where have you been, boy?" Pop asked when he saw me coming down the road. "I told you to help your mother this afternoon covering them plants with jars. We're likely to get a late frost tonight, and I don't want to lose them."

I had decided not to tell Pop or anyone about the monkey for fear they wouldn't believe me. But I was so excited I said, "I can't, Pop. I got to go catch the monkey I saw in the woods."

"Monkey?" he said. "What are you talking about?"

"I seen a monkey in the woods on the way home," I said. "Honest I did."

"Rosemary, this boy is dumber than we thought. There are no monkeys in Clay, you fool."

"I saw one, really I did. I got a good look at it."

"I bet you did," he said, looking away and throwing his cigarette butt down. "You stop your daydreaming and trying to get out of work and do what I said."

"But Pop . . ." I felt like I had cast my pearl before swine.

"You heard me."

When I turned around, I saw Mama standing there on the porch with a box of Mason jars.

"So you saw a monkey today, did you, Clarence?" She smiled, and I knew she didn't believe me either.

"I did, Mama, really I did," I said.

"Now, Clarence, I'd like to believe you, but how do you suppose a monkey came to live in these woods?" She walked closer, taking jars from the box and handing them to me.

"Maybe it escaped from the circus. It's true. You gotta believe me. First I thought it was a possum but it stood up on its hind legs and looked at me."

"Are you still stewing about not getting to go to the circus?" she asked. "Well, it's an odd thing, but if you say so, I guess it's true."

Pop came toward the porch when he heard what she was saying. "Don't you let that boy get away with telling lies."

"It's not really a lie, Addison, it's just a tale," she said.

"It's foolishness and I don't want to hear it. Next he'll be telling me there are giants living in the woods and he can't go to school or they'll eat him," he said.

I grabbed the Mason jars and ran off the porch and put them over all the plants in the garden. I couldn't help listening.

"Addie, why did you have to go and upset the boy? It doesn't hurt anything, him playing he saw a monkey," she said.

"He's too old for that now. He's almost grown."

He was right. There were other fourteen-year-old boys who'd already quit school to work in the mines. Mostly they worked outside, running errands and moving equipment. They had to be a full sixteen years old before they were allowed to work underground. But you could always find some mine operator who was desperate enough to hire them anyway, usually during strike time, when the regular men weren't on the line.

"Why, he's practically old enough to get a man's job," Pop said.

"I don't want him to get a man's job, at least not a miner's job. I want him to go to school, maybe even to college, not hang out around here all his life," Mama said.

"You think that boy could ever go to college?" Pop asked, like he had never thought of it before. Neither had I. The only people I knew that went to college were the teachers in the school. I didn't know much about college, just that if you went, you didn't have to come back and work in the mines. You didn't have to come back at all. The Rodricks from our church had sent their son away a couple of years before and he hadn't been back since.

"Clarence's grades aren't bad and he tries real hard," Mama answered. "I started a little savings for him."

"You didn't tell me that," Pop said. "I wondered where our extra money was going."

Henry and the other boys were bound to quit school and start work in the mines. Their families could use the money. I guess we could too. But Pop had never suggested I start. I guess he didn't really want me there after all.

That night after I finished my chores, I lay in bed looking out at the sky. I felt like I'd seen a star I had never seen before.

Chapter 16

I saw Johnny every day the next week, mostly at school. That Sunday he came to pass a football a little.

"I never knew you could throw," he said, catching.

"Sterling taught me." I reached up for his return.

"You don't even throw like a girl."

"Mother always says I should be more ladylike," I said, and whirled the ball as hard as I could, laughing.

He caught it easily. "I like you the way you are," he answered. "I don't like those girls who are brushing their hair and looking in the mirror all the time. You don't do that."

"Nope," I said. "Not me." Minutes before, I'd been in the bathroom pulling my hair back in a fancy clip.

He passed the football back. "I can't wait for next season. We didn't lose any real good seniors this year. I think we're going to have one of the strongest teams in the state."

"That'll be fun." I ran backward to make the catch.

"It'll be the best. I might get an offer to play football from a big college."

"Sterling's planning on college too, if he can get a scholarship," I said, and sent the ball back.

"I bet he will since he studies so hard." Johnny held the ball underneath his arm and smiled at me.

"Not that hard," I said.

"He's just smart," Johnny said.

"I've been wondering how smart he is lately."

"What's that supposed to mean?"

"Oh, I don't know. What will you study at college?"

"I just want to play football."

"I think I might study English and come back and be a teacher or a writer," I said.

"An English teacher? All that poetry and crap?" We started passing again.

"Don't you like the sonnets? Those beautiful love poems?"

"Poetry is for girls."

"I'm sure glad William Shakespeare didn't think that. What about 'Casey at the Bat'?"

"Maybe not *all* poetry is for girls. But I don't have much use for it."

"Poetry helps me understand what it's like to be in love or be in a battle or just to notice the beauty of the spring."

Johnny walked toward me with the ball under his arm. "You remind me of Mrs. Anderson. All we did was read those poems in her class. Maybe in ten years that's what people will be saying about your class."

"I hope so."

"I can't believe you'd want to come back here. Why?"

" 'Cause it's my home."

"I don't know why anybody would want to live here," he said. "There's a world out there with lots to do besides mining or selling machinery. That's what my dad wants me to do."

"What would you rather do?"

"Probably coach football or something. But I aim to get out of here."

"Wouldn't you miss the mountains, the peacefulness of climbing in the woods by yourself?"

"What's to miss? There isn't anything to do around here," he said.

"I want to see the world too. First, I'd love to go to Paris and see the Eiffel Tower. But then I want to come back, to have a place to call home where people know me."

"I don't know about Paris. I'd just like to go to Charleston. I think they got a couple big high schools there where I could coach and get out of this town."

We stopped passing for a while and sat together on the porch stoop. His wrist rubbed against mine and I could smell his sweat.

I looked across the road into the trees and up the

hillside. It was the edge of night. The air had cooled, bringing goose bumps to my skin. It was the time when creatures began calling one another, the whippoorwills and then the frogs and the owls and the crickets. They made the noises of the night, the ones that lulled me to sleep, the ones I never wanted to be without.

"What do you think is going to happen to the town if there's a strike?" I asked.

"They practically got an armory down in those tents. Whatever happens, someone is sure to get killed."

"No! Do you really think so?"

"You don't get men together with guns and expect nobody to get hurt."

"Not Sterling or Daddy or anyone else we know! I hope it isn't anyone at all."

"I do too. But Sterling is sure putting himself in the middle of things."

"That's what worries me," I said. Johnny picked up a rock and tossed it in his hands. "Think I can hit that rock?" He pointed to a huge stone that forced the road to bend.

"I bet you can."

"You're supposed to say I can't."

"Is that the way it goes?"

"That way I can impress you when I hit it."

"I'll remember that next time," I told him, giggling. He threw the rock, but it bounced before it hit the stone.

"Oh, well," I laughed.

"I'll get it next time," he said, so determined it made me smile.

"Can I walk you to school tomorrow?" he said.

"Sure. But you don't want to come all the way out here."

"I'll meet you halfway."

"Okay."

"See you then." He tipped his hand to me, like a soldier saluting, and walked away.

After he left, I sat out on the porch just thinking about all the things he'd said. I could see him in ten years, standing on the sidelines of a football field screaming commands at all the players. If someone had ever been born for something, it was Johnny for that. Me, I didn't care a lick about football and I never would.

Hattie came out and plopped down beside me. "How's your boyfriend?"

"I don't know if he's really my boyfriend."

"Did he kiss you?"

"That's none of your business."

"So he did. And that means he's your boyfriend. Are you in love with him? You walk around talking to yourself all the time, looking dreamy."

"I like him. He's funny. I like going on dates, having a boy to talk to. Sally talks about it all the time, going to movies and to the drugstore."

"I wish I could go on a date."

"You will. You have plenty of time. You'll have lots of dates because you're so pretty."

"Do you really think I'm pretty?"

"Of course," I answered.

"You're pretty too."

"Really?"

"You girls better be getting to bed. You've got school in the morning," Mother said.

Hattie pushed herself up and went inside.

"I think I'll sit just a bit longer," I said. Johnny's attention made me feel like I could do anything I wanted. I thought about girls who were like I was before I met Johnny, girls no one noticed. I hadn't realized how lonely I was before. How lonely they must be! It wasn't fair.

All this made me think of Clarence. I wondered if anyone would ever like him the way Johnny liked me.

Chapter 17

Johnny walked me to school all week. On Friday in homeroom, Sally said, "You and Johnny must be going steady by now."

I shrugged.

"What's that supposed to mean? Are you or not? Tell me in science," she said. I managed to avoid her there too. I knew I couldn't avoid her forever, but I didn't know what to say. I was embarassed. What would I say if he were to ask me?

After school I stood on the sidewalk by the flag-pole, waiting for Hattie. Angela saw me. "You're going to the drugstore with us, aren't you?"

"I never go to the drugstore. Why would I go today?"

"I just thought that since you and Johnny were an item you'd be going to the drugstore on Fridays like the rest of us."

"An item?" I laughed. "I usually walk home with Hattie."

"Oh, can't someone else walk her home? Come and see if Irv will ask me to the dance. He always hangs out there on Fridays with the rest of the guys. Besides, Johnny will be there."

Hattie stood beside me, tapping her foot impatiently.

"He will? He didn't say anything to me about it. I don't think I want to just show up."

"Why not?"

"I've never been there after school before. Johnny might think I'm following him or something."

"What's the matter? He seems crazy about you."

"Hattie might mind if I didn't walk her home."

"I thought you liked Johnny." Angela turned to me.

"I do."

"Then come on."

"What are you guys talking 'bout?" Sally came up from behind.

"I'm trying to get Elizabeth to come to the drugstore. I think Irv might ask me to the dance."

Sally laughed. "Elizabeth, you're just playing hard to get with Johnny."

"I am not. I have to walk Hattie home."

"I don't mind going if you buy me something," Hattie said.

"No, come on." I pulled her along with a wink and Sally and Angela turned to go.

"Wait up!" Sterling jogged to catch us.

"How come you aren't going to the drugstore with the girls?" Hattie said.

"I didn't feel like it."

"Sally and Angela were trying to get Elizabeth to go to the drugstore, but she said she had to walk me home," Hattie said to Sterling. "They said she was just playing hard to get."

"Ha! Were you?" Sterling fell into step behind us.

"It isn't like that. It's hard to explain."

"Try," Sterling said.

"I don't even know why Johnny likes me. I'm not like those other girls."

"Maybe that's why he likes you."

"It's funny. Since I got to high school, I've dreamed about going to the drugstore and hanging out with the football team and all the pretty girls. But I don't think I would have that much fun after all."

"I know what you mean," said Sterling. "You ain't the type."

The day of the dance, we were all busy putting up decorations in the gym. We decided to hang red, white and blue streamers and balloons all through the lights on the ceiling.

"Aren't you excited?" Angela asked. "I tossed and turned all night just thinking about tonight. I know

I'm a sight today. I tried putting cucumbers underneath my eyes to get rid of these black bags, but I don't think it helped much. I'm so afraid Irv will take one look at me and run the other way."

"Oh, Angela, you look fine," Sally said.

"Poor Mary O'Dell has to go with Sam Waters. He's such a goof," Angela said. We tied bows on the window shades.

"Oh, you know Mary," I said, "she'll have fun anyway."

"Are you going to do anything different with your hair?" Sally asked me. "I saw a French twist in a magazine. I suppose you're going to tie yours back as usual."

"I might do something different," I answered, not really meaning it. It was going to be bad enough going out in a fancy dress. If I tried to do anything fancy with my hair, Sterling and Hattie would tease me no end.

"Elizabeth, I'm sorry for what I said to you last week, about you and Johnny not really fitting together. Well, I've been watching you all together and I can see that Johnny is just crazy about you."

"I don't know. If he is, I don't really understand why."

"I didn't at first either—no offense—but now I do."

"Tell me." I turned around on the ladder to look at her.

"My cousin in Hollywood is all the time telling me not to be so obviously boy-crazy. She says girls that are more aloof are really more alluring."

"I'm not trying to be aloof."

"I know. You're just quiet naturally. I tried to be more like you. I pretended I didn't even notice Sterling, but he still didn't talk to me. How come he isn't going to the dance, anyway?"

"Sterling can't seem to think of anything but the union."

"My papa says if he catches a union man on his property he'll shoot him dead," Angela said.

"My daddy doesn't like them either," I said, "but Sterling has practically joined up." Sally handed me more bows to hang while Angela steadied the ladder.

"Is your father going to kick him out of the house?" Sally asked.

"He'd never do that," I said.

"Well, my dad is practically living at the union tent. My mother takes food down there every day. Sometimes I go with her," Sally said.

"Now we know why Sterling hangs out there so much," Angela said, laughing.

"I went to the union meeting a couple weeks ago," I said.

"You did not," Sally said. "They don't let girls go."

"I went with Sterling. You would have liked it too, 'cause there was a handsome guy that did all the talking. Tony was his name."

"What did you think?" Angela asked. "Were they crazy?"

"Not like I thought. The way my daddy talks, those men are as bad as the devil himself. But I could see why Sterling likes them. This Tony fellow seemed to want to help people. He didn't seem bad at all. But then the other night, a bunch of these union fellows put a noose around Mr. Murphy's neck! Like to scared him to death! I don't know what to think."

"My daddy said if they had done that to him none of them would be alive to tell about it," Angela said.

"The union men I've met aren't cruel like that. They have kids and they came to help our families," Sally said.

"Let's just hope there's no trouble tonight. I finally get a date with Irv and all this nonsense could mess things up," Angela said.

Chapter 18

"Mother, are you really going to let Elizabeth go? I thought we weren't allowed to dance," Hattie asked.

"I don't suppose it will hurt anything. Even the Israelites danced," Mother said.

"But she is still a Baptist, isn't she?" Grandma said. Mother just smiled at her.

"Mother, don't let her wear my shoes all over this house. She'll get them dirty." Hattie had spent the last hour tromping around in my fancy shoes.

My dress was a little too big and I stood in front of the mirror pulling at the sides of the skirt. "I look like a child playing dress-up."

"You look right smart," Mother said. "That lavender is so pretty with your skin. Now hold still while I tie your sash." Mother had got the dress at the clothes exchange. It was a real party dress with a satin sash. No one knew how it wound up in Clay County. Mother had come home from the exchange and held it up.

"This dress," she'd said, "is for a real special young lady."

It had cost her more than she would say, but Daddy said his daughter deserved the best. Only a handful of girls would have on a new dress. Most girls wore their Sunday best and borrowed shoes. There were lots too poor to do even that. The poorest wouldn't have a chance to go to the dance anyway, like Alma Jarrel. She and I had been best friends up to the third grade. She lived in the company town with her brothers and sisters. They had newspapers for wallpaper, which I thought was kind of neat until I realized it meant she was really poor. Alma's daddy coughed all the time and had a lung condition. On account of him being sick, she had quit school after eighth grade to find work. I saw her and her mom waiting for coal trucks to pass so they could gather the chunks that fell off. Lots of people did that in the winter, but Alma and her mom did it all year long. I looked at my dress and I wondered what Alma would think of me now.

Mother put powder on my shoulders to make them look silky smooth. "You're blushing," she teased me.

"I reckon you're going to be the prettiest girl at that dance," Daddy said. "Before you go off with some high school boy you'd better give your old dad a whirl around here."

Mother fiddled with the dial on the radio until she found the one music station.

"You old silly goose, what are you dancing for?" Grandma said to Daddy, and screwed up her nose.

"She does look lovely, doesn't she, Grandma?" Daddy said.

"That she does. I just don't approve of dancing."

We watched John Beasley get out of his truck with his daddy's black coat on and his hair slicked back. Sterling's face went sour with regret when he saw Johnny coming to the door.

"You ain't going to be the prettiest girl there," Sterling said. "Sally Jennings is."

"If she's so pretty, why aren't you taking her?" Hattie asked.

"I'm going into town for a meeting since it's the first night of the strike."

"You heard what I said about them meetings," Daddy said.

"And Sterling, you know we don't want you around that kind of people." Mother marched right up to him.

"Some of them union men used to be your friends," Sterling said. "They ain't a bunch of outsiders like you said."

My hands were clenched around Mother's arm. "Not now," I muttered.

"Hush," Mother said. "Here comes Johnny. This is Elizabeth's special night."

"Evening, Mr. and Mrs. Braxton," Johnny said.

"You look mighty nice, John Beasley," Mother said.

Johnny bit his lower lip and looked at me shyly. "I like your dress."

"Thanks," I said. "Well, I guess we'll go on now."

"Be back by ten o'clock," Daddy said.

"Yes sir," said Johnny. "Don't worry about a thing. I'll take good care of her." He put out his arm for me to hold, and I held it tightly even though I knew my whole family's eyes were upon us.

"Boy, I want you to come with me tonight to the union meeting and see what all this is about."

"What are you taking Clarence for?" Mama asked. She had already started doing dishes while Pop and me finished up some rhubarb pie at the table. "Folks are talking about shooting and all. Sarah is on standby in case anyone gets hurt." Sarah was the town operator, who took all the messages for the sheriff.

"You got to stop babying this boy. He's going to grow up to be a sissy. It ain't going to be us that's getting hurt, it'll be those damn scabs if they cross the picket lines tonight. We gave them a warning. If any of those men come to work after midnight tonight, there'll be trouble," Pop said.

"What kind of trouble?" she asked.

"It ain't for me to say."

"Addie, all this talk scares me. None of this is worth anyone getting killed over. Please don't go."

"I'll be all right so long as I got my rifle."

"Rifle? Do you have to take that along? Hate begets hate, Addie. What will happen to me if you go and get yourself killed?"

"Better to be killed quickly than this slow death in the mines. Unions are the answer, just wait and see," he said. Then he put on his hat and turned toward the door.

"Let Clarence stay home tonight," Mama said. "He can go with you another night."

"But Mama," I said, "I want to go."

Pop looked at me and looked back at her and said, "You stay here." He didn't give me a reason. I think it was because I said I wanted to go. Sometimes I'd have sworn he hated me.

Pop walked out the door carrying his rifle, more determined than ever.

"Your pop looks like he's going off to war," Mama said. "I just wish I knew whose side I was on."

"You mean you ain't on Pop's side?" I asked.

"It isn't that I'm not on your pop's side. I understand how a man feels when he's not treated like a human being. But if things are so bad, why aren't good people like Elizabeth's father, Ezra, involved? I've known Ezra Braxton all my life, and he is anything but a coward."

113

Chapter 19

"Stop it," I told Johnny when he sang "Sixteen and in Love" in my ear loud enough for people to hear. He laughed when I turned my head away from him. He liked making me blush. I felt the glares of some of the senior girls hot on my back.

"She's not that pretty," I'd heard one mutter when we came in.

"I didn't know who she was until a couple of weeks ago," whispered her friend. I gripped Johnny's hand even tighter and smiled at them.

He wrapped his arm around me. "Let's walk out back. I need some fresh air." I had watched other couples stray out the gym's back door all evening. Mr. Hodgekins stood close to the door and made sure people weren't gone too long, just enough for a kiss or two. Sally winked at me as we passed her.

It was cool outside and smelled of newly cut grass. Someone had left a candle on the steps. It flickered when the door shut. Johnny took off his coat and wrapped it around me. The warmth of his body lingered inside. He pulled me to a bench and we sat down.

"I've been thinking. Coach says he's certain I'll get a football scholarship to West Virginia. Maybe you could come visit me sometimes."

"Oh, that would be fun."

"They have big dances. You could stay with my cousin. All I mean is that I think I'd like to be around you for a long time." He paused. I didn't know what to say.

"I love you, Elizabeth," he said, looking into my eyes.

I could feel my face flushing so I lowered my chin. He pulled it up with his finger and kissed me. I kissed him back. I wanted to say that I loved him, because I knew it was what he wanted, but I said, "Johnny, you silly thing, why, that's a whole year away and you'll probably have forgotten about me by then. It's real sweet of you to say that anyway."

When he looked into my eyes, all I knew was that I loved the idea of him, the attention, the feel of his hand in mine. But I didn't think I really loved him. I couldn't give such a thing away so easily, the way other girls did. He reached for my hand. I slipped it into his and followed him back inside.

* * *

We weren't more than fifteen minutes late, but Daddy was standing at the door waiting and looking troubled.

He stood there in his work boots, Thermos in hand. The hoot owl shift began at eleven o'clock, and Daddy always worked that shift on Friday so that he could be home on Saturday to help with the chores.

"Come on in, Johnny, and have a cup of coffee," Mother yelled from the porch.

At least *she* was friendly.

"I don't expect you'd better, son," Daddy sighed. "There's a lot of men with an itchy trigger finger, and you being up this way too late at night, they might think you were crossing the picket line. You'd better get home."

"I suspect you're right."

Daddy stepped inside the door long enough for Johnny to kiss me goodnight. I felt my insides well up and my legs weaken. I didn't want to stop, but he pulled away and held my face in his hands for a few minutes and stroked my cheek with his thumb. He looked more handsome than ever. Why didn't I love him?

He stepped back and looked off the porch.

"All this time and I never knew your daddy was a scab."

"What!" The words hit me like a slap.

"With you and Sterling going to the union meetings, I just figured your daddy was union too."

116

"He isn't a scab!"

"He's planning to cross the picket lines, isn't he?"

"He's going to go to work, if that's what you mean."

"Then that makes him a scab," he said.

"What does it matter to you?"

"Well, I guess it doesn't, except everybody knows that there ain't nothing lower than a scab."

I dropped my hand from his. "How can you talk about my father that way? He's never done anything to hurt you. Your own daddy makes his money selling to Mr. Bagby."

"That doesn't make him a scab. I'm only saying what I know, Elizabeth."

"If that's the way you feel, then I don't want to have anything to do with you, John Beasley," I said. I backed into the house and slammed the door.

Mother was just inside.

"Did you two have a quarrel?" she asked, and peered at my face, streaked with tears.

I shook my head. "Can I sit out on the porch a bit?"

"Don't be long. Your father is fixing to leave and he'll want you in before he goes."

I waited until I heard Johnny slam his truck door. He must have been pretty mad at me, but he deserved it. He had no right to talk that way. I stood just inside the door, wondering what to do. Mother always said to never let the sun go down on your anger. If I went to bed angry with Johnny, I wouldn't be able to sleep.

Besides, my own brother might have thought the same thing about Daddy being a scab. I opened the door and saw Johnny's truck still parked outside. He must have been feeling bad too. I walked over to the window.

"I'm sorry I slammed the door in your face."

"I don't blame you," he said, looking at me and then away. "I shouldn't have said that about your father. You're strong-headed." He looked at me and smiled.

"I had a wonderful time tonight."

"Me too. But I suspect your daddy is right. I best be getting home."

"Good night, Johnny," I said. He reached out the window and squeezed the top of my shoulder. I put my hand on top of his.

"Good night." He winked and drove away.

I went straight to my room, slipped off my dress and laid it over the chair. Hattie slept soundly, leaving me the quiet of the room to think about the night. I sat in the dark a long time. The dance, the air, the music, the ride now felt like a dream. I tried not to think about Johnny calling Daddy a scab but only about kissing him and seeing the look on his face when he told me good night. I got in bed and lay awake, reliving every moment of the dance, thinking of the jealous girls I did not know and the smiles of Sally and Angela.

Grandma was sitting up late, and Mother sat with her. She never felt uneasy the way Grandma did, but she trusted Grandma's feelings like they were her own.

As I began to fall asleep, I heard Mother say, "Ezra, what are you doing home?" My eyes opened wide in the dark. I knew it instantly, even before he'd finished speaking.

"There's been an accident."

"What do you mean?" Mother asked.

"It's Johnny Beasley. He's hurt bad."

"What!" Grandma said.

I rushed from my room.

"What happened?" I screamed.

Daddy came toward me and bent down on one knee.

"I'm sorry," he said, throwing his arms around me.

"Will he be all right?"

"I don't know," he answered. I felt my head tilt back and my body heave and heard my voice cry out.

It was a while before I could even breathe, before I could hear Daddy tell what happened.

Daddy had decided to meet a few of his friends so that they could walk together in case there was trouble.

They had made it to the first house in the hollow when they heard the sheriff's siren coming down the hill. It echoed between the deep cuts of the mountain, its red light flashing, disturbing the dense fog of the night. The men jogged toward the cars ahead. Then Daddy saw Johnny's truck.

The train had stopped about a hundred feet after ramming it. Daddy rushed over to Johnny and heard the conductor crying, "I didn't know it was a boy! I thought it was the strikers baiting me, trying to stop the coal trucks. I had no idea it was a kid. I thought he was going to move, but he just sat there waving at me. By the time I realized his car had stalled, it was too late." The conductor put his hands over his face and sobbed. Daddy touched Johnny's wrist and felt a slight pulse.

"Hey," he hollered, "this boy's still alive! Let's get him out of here." The conductor and the other miners started using their shovels to pull apart the wreckage while Daddy ran up the hill toward the mine to get more men and better equipment.

"The rest is up to God and the doctors in Charleston," Daddy said. "It'll be another hour before they make it to the hospital."

"Jesus, Jesus," Mother said over and over when Daddy finished. "Come here, girl." I wrapped my arms around her and crawled into her lap.

"It can't be. He just kissed me."

"I don't know if he's going to make it," Daddy said. Sterling sat in a chair, his elbows in his lap, his hands holding his head. Everyone but Grandma cried. Mother prayed.

"He won't die, Mother, I know he won't," I said. I pleaded with God too, but I was scared. If Johnny didn't die, he might lose everything he was hoping for—the scholarship and college and the coaching job. He might never get to play football again.

Grandma made some coffee and Daddy stirred up the fire. Hattie kept sobbing but I tried to hold back the tears, like keeping them back might keep him alive. But I couldn't escape their taste on my lips.

"The strike hadn't even started and look what happened," Mother said. I stood up with a shiver and went to my room.

Hattie got up to follow me, but Mother said, "Hattie, leave her be. We all need to be alone with God. He's the only one that can save that boy now."

Chapter 20

"Elizabeth?" Sterling called softly so as not to wake anyone who might still be asleep. It was just after dawn.

"I'm on the porch."

"Did you sleep?" he asked.

"Not too much."

"Let's go into town and see what's going on."

The drive to town was so long; everything seemed different. My eyes were dry and tired. Sterling didn't say anything the whole way.

Sterling's friends were sitting in a line at the drugstore. They all sidled up to the truck when they saw us.

"Johnny ain't doing good," Charlie Avery said. "His daddy came back from Charleston at three in the morning to bring his mom down there."

"That scab conductor," Harry Avis said. "He wanted to kill someone."

"You can't blame him," Sterling answered. "It was

the dadblamed unions. Everybody knows they block railroads all the time. How was he to know?"

"I thought you were union," Harry said.

"I don't know what I am. I just want Johnny to be all right," Sterling said. We were all quiet, keeping our eyes on anything but one another.

Johnny died that afternoon.

When Harry came with the news, I ran straight to my spot in the woods. I half expected it not to be there, some storm having blown it away, but the moss spread out before me soft as a chick's down. The thrush flittered around, announcing my presence, while a few squirrels scampered above me in the tips of the trees just like Johnny hadn't died at all.

It was my fault. I'd made him mad. Maybe he hadn't been thinking clearly and had stalled. I sank to my knees and thought my heart would break open.

It was hard to think. I'd cry a while, then laugh at something Johnny had said, then cry again. I'd think of all the girls feeling sorry for me and get mad at myself for feeling sorry for myself when really it was Johnny and his family I ought to be feeling sorry for. I'd been the last to see him, to touch him, to hold his hand. Had I said the things I should have? Had his last evening been fine? If only I'd told him that I loved him. But Johnny had faced that train alone and afraid. That was the worst part.

Every time I thought the tears were gone and I was ready to go back home, they'd begin again. I'd never known anyone who died so young. Daddy's brother, Randolph, had been killed in a mine collapse a few years back. All I remembered was the quiet that fell over the house. We'd hardly laughed or talked for days, even about normal things. After a time, life had gone back to the way things used to be. But not this time. I couldn't imagine how I would ever feel normal again. Every time I'd go to school, I'd think of him. *Oh, Johnny, how will I go on?*

When I finally went home, Mother was standing on the porch waiting. She pulled me to her until her arms wrapped around my shoulders. I stayed there a long time.

"Come on inside an' eat something," she said.

"I'm not hungry."

"I know, but it'll do you good."

I sat at the table waiting for a piece of toast. Grandma watched me. I hated it when she just stared that way. It was like she knew what I was thinking.

She had told a story to me and Hattie when we were little and didn't know about love. She had a baby sister named Agnes who had been engaged to Cornet, a tall, dark-haired fellow, Gypsy-like and romantic. His family was black Irish, and farmed the north side of the county. She met him at a church picnic and knew she'd love him forever. One cold day, his mare slipped on a patch of ice and threw him. He landed on a rock and took an infection from which he never recovered. The mare had to be shot. That was the part of the story Hattie remembered most.

"Couldn't they save the horse?" she asked. Grandma answered patiently, but the question must have troubled her. Agnes was much younger than Grandma, more like a daughter to her than a sister. Her pain was Grandma's pain. Agnes never married, but grieved for Cornet every year on the anniversary of his death. After Agnes died, Grandma kept up her tradition. I remember her walking up to the mountain where Cornet was buried. The year before, she'd asked Sterling to take her, said her bones were aching and she needed someone to steady her. She laid a rose on his grave. It was a simple headstone with just his name and the years of his birth and death with an inscription underneath that read THIS MONUMENT WAS ERECTED BY THOSE WHO WILL NEVER CEASE TO MOURN HIS LOSS.

Life wasn't hard or easy for Grandma; life just was. I was sitting on my bed rolling a handkerchief over in my hands when she came to me.

"You'll get through this. Overcoming heartache is sort of like climbing a mountain of molasses. Sometimes you feel stuck there, with the darkness surrounding you, tugging at your feet and pulling you down. But other times, things are sweet and you can see your way to go on." Wrinkles rippled out from the corners of her mouth and the rims of her tired eyes. I could tell she'd made it up her share of molasses mountains.

"The climbing will help you appreciate life."

I feared I didn't have her kind of strength.

Chapter 21

Everybody in town had loved Johnny and been mighty proud of him. They had hoped he'd make a name for himself and for them, away from here.

The churches were packed full that Sunday. Even Chester French went to church, and he hadn't been since his wife died some twenty years before. Our preacher took advantage of the perfect attendance to give a sermon on reconciliation. He said that in a way, Johnny was like Jesus, his innocent blood shed for the sins of union and nonunion alike. He called on all those parties in the conflict to let Johnny's death reconcile them so that his death would not have been in vain. Many took it to heart, and there was a reckless hope that the strike would end.

Johnny's funeral was Monday morning. They had his coffin at the town funeral home Sunday night. Mother had sent a ham for the family Saturday night. Folks were good that way. In fact, if it was the woman of the house that passed, you could be sure the men were taken care of until they married again or learned to fend for themselves, which seemed to take a lot longer than it should.

All the girls hovered around me, trying to share in my grief and attention. They were truly sad for me and for themselves. I wished I could tell them all my fears and doubts about Johnny, but I was too afraid. The only person I could bear was Sally; she didn't talk, she just sat with me. I couldn't let go of her hand.

"I'm glad Johnny's last evening was with a sweet girl like you," his mother said to me. It made me cry, but not for the reason she thought.

Johnny's face was all made up and he didn't look anything like himself. They had combed his hair and slicked it to the side in a way he would have hated, but everyone said, "Doesn't he look nice and peaceful." He looked sad to me. I wondered if that was because he had seen the train coming and the fear that had gripped him slid out of his body and settled into sadness for losing his life so young.

Grown boys broke down bawling. Nothing the preacher said, nothing anybody said really calmed them. Mother put her arm around me and reached over to touch Sterling's shoulder. He was crying too, using Daddy's handkerchief.

Clarence and his family sat in front of us. His mother took a tissue to her eyes while the preacher talked, but Clarence looked like he always did, staring down at his shoes.

When we got home, Grandma motioned for me to sit beside her. I dried my face.

"It's okay to cry now," she said, and something about her voice brought the tears again.

"Grief settled in a girl your age is only bad. That's what tears are for. If you hold them back, patches of grief might never wash out. Just like blackberry stains, the sooner you wash them, the better."

Chapter 22

We went to Johnny's funeral. But I didn't cry the way everybody else did. I just kept remembering the mean things he'd said or the times he wouldn't look at me at all. That didn't keep me from being a little sad. I felt the most sorry for his mama. Her shoulders heaved up and down the whole service.

Johnny died a few days before school was out. No one went those last days. I was happy to be away from all the kids; I'd have more time to catch that monkey. If I could catch it, maybe Pop would let me keep it. Maybe I could even train it to do chores around the house. One thing was for sure, no one else I knew would have a monkey.

After the accident, the union activity stopped for a while. Pop didn't talk much about the strike for a few days. But before long, he said to me, "Every miner out of work is in those woods hunting. You'd better watch out, sneaking around like you do. You're likely to get yourself kilt."

I was more worried about that monkey than myself. Those men would shoot at anything. I headed out to the dump, close to where I'd seen it climbing in the trees. I picked up a couple of tin cans that had been newly splattered with shotgun holes to eye them closer. When I did, I heard a noise, a high-pitched *eeck* like I'd heard the day I saw Johnny Beasley kiss Elizabeth. It was watching me, still flashing that mirror around to catch the sun.

There was a pawpaw patch not far away, so I stole over to get one. I tossed it up, hoping the monkey would catch it. But I only made it more nervous. It climbed back and forth on a limb, its tail feeling the branches above.

"Come on, I won't hurt you."

I held the pawpaw in my hand and walked toward the tree. An old crate made me tall enough to place the fruit in the fork of the tree and wait for the monkey to come. I knew what it was like for someone to get too close.

After a while, it came down and began biting the fruit. I couldn't believe my eyes. Its tail was long and flipped around like a squirrel's. It spit the seeds right at me and seemed to laugh about it. I crouched down so it could see my face.

"Don't be afraid," I told it. "I ain't going to hurt you. You probably haven't seen anyone that looks like me before. Have you? It's all right." It looked in my eyes and studied me awhile. As soon as I moved my hand toward the limb, it rushed up the tree, carrying what was left of the pawpaw.

I didn't see it again for a couple days. Mother had made a blackberry cobbler for dessert one evening, and I was sitting out on the porch enjoying it like nothing else. It was her first of the year and it was the tastiest I remembered. That was when I got an idea. If I was happiest eating my favorite food, then I guessed the monkey would be too. Maybe then I could get close enough to catch it.

"Could I buy the bananas that are gone bad?" I asked Mr. Sampson at the grocery. Fresh bananas were too expensive.

"I don't have but a few and, well, what would you want to do a fool thing like that for?" he asked.

"My mama uses them for banana bread," I answered, thinking fast.

"I suppose I can sell you a few, but why didn't your mother get them when she came in a little while ago?"

"I reckon she forgot."

"I don't feel right about selling these to you. Just take them," he said.

"My pop would get upset if I took something without paying for it."

"I suppose you're right." He gave me three rotten bananas and I held out a dime.

"Thank you," I said.

I had gone to the library the day before to look at an encyclopedia.

"Why, Clarence," the librarian said, "I never knew you to be fond of books, or reading."

"I like reading. I'll just use the encyclopedia."

"Suit yourself."

The monkey I had seen looked like one that came from Asia. The encyclopedia said they were greedy, which made trapping easy. If you put a banana in a jar, the monkey would put his hand inside and not let go even though his clenched fist was too big to get out of the jar.

I stuffed the bananas in a bag. The rain made walking quieter, so I approached the dump without making any noise. No one was there. I found a Mason jar with the lid rusted through and stuck the banana down inside. I took it to the base of the tree and wedged it in so the monkey couldn't walk away with the whole thing. Sure enough, the monkey came down branch by branch while I watched from afar. I had spied an old crate the day before and set it aside for a cage. Later I could build it a much bigger cage hidden far away.

When it neared the base of the tree, it sat up on its back legs watching me, like it knew I was going to catch it. It stuck its hand inside the jar anyway. And just like the encyclopedia said, it began screeching and

133

pulling at the banana. I ran over and threw the crate over it.

I looked inside. "It's okay," I told it. The banana was mushy and the monkey pulled its hand out and licked at its fingers like I might have done with Mama's icing. I took a piece of board and slid it underneath and carefully turned the crate over. I could feel the monkey hopping around when I heard a hum of sounds coming up the road. It was Henry and his friends. I grabbed the box, held the board tight on top and ran up the hill as fast as I could. Branches lashed against my face. Henry and his friends were too busy arguing to see me, even though I wasn't yet over the hill when they began shooting tin cans.

I was shaking from nervousness and the damp air when I reached the top of the hill. I feared lifting the board from the top of the crate, so I kept it shut and peeked through the wooden slats. Its fingers were thin like an old woman's and grabbed at mine to play. When I heard shooting, I walked again, hoping they would think I was some animal trying to scurry away.

The cave wasn't but two hills over from the dump, yet by the time I reached it, I was wore out. I laid the crate upside down so I could see the monkey better. With my knife, I cut stakes and used the rope in my box to secure its cage until I knew it'd trust me. The banana in my bag had mashed some, but the monkey took it from my hand just like a kid after candy.

It was a girl monkey. "It's okay," I told her. I could

see her fur stretched across her ribs. I decided to call her Cheetah.

"You're hungry, I know. I'm going to get you bananas every day if you want them, and I'll get you berries too." I stood at the mouth of the cave and noticed a berry bush just outside, which I had never noticed before. It was filled with the plumpest blackberries on the hill. It was a good sign.

Chapter 23

I didn't understand why Johnny had died, why God couldn't have stopped the train, or if he could have, why he hadn't. Mother says some questions take a lifetime to answer and some will be answered only when we see God. I wasn't sure I could wait that long.

The summer was usually filled with chores, but Mother didn't yell at me to do them. Hattie and Sterling, much to my surprise, pitched in and did more than their share for a while. It wasn't too long before I heard Hattie complain.

"How long do I have to do chores for Elizabeth?"

"As long as she needs you to."

"It's been more than two weeks. Don't you think she should be getting over this now?"

"Give her all the time she needs."

I wanted to stand up and scream, "I'm not grieving over Johnny anymore!" but it was too much to explain. I did miss him. I missed how he'd made me feel, how he'd changed everything. I missed seeing his face and the way he'd looked at me. And I troubled over him being gone from the world, not just gone from me. But I was not heartbroken like they thought. I was mad, mad at God.

I went to my special spot in the woods to try to sort things out. Some days I'd just sit there and other days I'd write the whole time. Johnny's death did something to my thinking, unsettled my mind; everything I'd once thought sure was now uncertain. If Johnny could die, why couldn't I? Why couldn't anyone at any time? Was there nothing I could be sure of? I guess I was writing all these questions to God. If he was all-powerful, like the preacher said, why did he allow little children and someone like Johnny to suffer or die? Why couldn't everyone die like my grandmother's sister? Her long life ended one Christmas night. Grandma and I had been tending to her for days. After Christmas dinner we went to check on her. I hadn't wanted to go. I wanted to stay home and admire all my presents, but Grandma needed me to stoke the stove. When we entered her cabin, we saw Aunt Ida fixed in her chair, its fabric molded to her body. She didn't acknowledge our presence except for a slight swaying. While Grandma tried to feed her, I brought the wood in. Then we sat and watched the fire. We didn't even realize she had closed her eyes and was gone until we got up to leave. It was the way I imagined everyone would die.

I thought about Clarence walking along by himself. Why was he so cursed? Weren't there rewards for goodness in life? If a person was good, shouldn't good things happen to him? What had Clarence done to be treated so cruelly by everyone? Why did he have to be alone all the time?

Sunday came around and I told Mother I didn't want to go to church.

"Church will do you good."

"Please don't make me go."

"I'll never make you go," she said. "Just don't turn away from God when you're hurting. Turn toward him."

Chapter 24

"Clarence, where have you been lately?" Mama asked one evening during supper. "I can hardly get you to do anything anymore."

"What do you mean?" Pop asked. "He's doing his chores, ain't he?"

"He is, but I don't see hide nor hair of him until dinner," she said. They talked as if I wasn't even there.

"Well, what have you got to say, boy?" Pop asked.

"I've just been hanging out in the woods is all, nothing special." I cleared the plates to help Mama, and when I took in the last one, she touched my arm. Pop had gone out back to smoke.

"Clarence," she said, "Mr. Sampson asked me if he could have a slice of my banana bread. He said you told him it was mighty tasty."

I stood quiet. Could she have seen me with Cheetah?

"I guess I kind of looked at him funny 'cause then he said, 'You know, the bananas that Clarence has been getting every day so you can make bread.' 'Yes, Mr. Sampson. I'll have to send you some,' I said." She looked at me and waited for me to say something. I only sighed, relieved.

"Now, Clarence, I am not one to lie. I don't want this to happen again. It's a good thing your pop doesn't know about you telling stories. If you're getting hungry, Clarence, you don't need to be eating rotten bananas. We aren't that poor," she said. She turned away from me and began running water in the sink.

"I know you're worried because Pop is out of work, but I don't want you eating any old bananas. I just had to take the hem out of your overalls. You must be hitting a growth spurt or something."

"I'm sorry," I said. She winked at me and smiled.

"I'll bake you some of that banana bread if you want," she said. "I guess I'll have to bake some for Mr. Sampson anyhow."

Cheetah stayed every morning in her cage waiting for me to come and let her out. As soon as I finished chores, I'd run to the cave. I didn't like having to keep her there alone, but it was safe. The first time I let her out of the crate, she near scared me to death. I expected her to run away, so I left some cookies at the edge of the cave. She darted out and jumped right on my shoulder like she had been trained. She could probably have done lots of tricks if I could have just figured out the way to ask her. She was smart enough to take coins from my pocket or cookies from my lunch bag. I thought of all the places I'd take her—to school and the drugstore, everywhere I'd go. Then when people'd stare, they wouldn't be staring 'cause I was ugly but 'cause I was something special with a monkey on my shoulder.

Over the next couple of weeks, she grew used to me and would climb trees alongside me while I walked. I stayed up on the hill or took the back path down to the creek to get her some water. But we tried never to cross the roads or railroad tracks. Mountain laurel and ivy were easy cover in case we heard someone coming.

We passed the days together. By the afternoon, she didn't seem to mind when I closed her in the cage. But in the mornings, she'd gotten used to my coming right before lunch and would screech and cry for me until I got there. I'd heard her calling clear from the dump last time.

"You can't be making that noise, girl," I told her. "Why, someone is likely to be walking by and hear you. Now, you wouldn't want that, would you?"

I tore up my arms good cutting big branches from a briar bush to camouflage the cave. I dug holes for the sticks to make them look rooted. No one would go through a thicket of briars even if they did hear some strange noise.

"You be real quiet now, you hear?" I think she

understood, but I didn't blame her for cackling. She was lonely without me, just like I was without her.

As soon as I had laid the last branch in place, I heard the crack of a stick breaking. I sat still like a hunted animal.

"Who's with you, Clarence?" It was Elizabeth. "Who are you talking to?" I didn't answer for a minute. My heart sank. Then Cheetah cackled.

"What in the world is that?" She was standing on the other side of the rock ledge and couldn't see into the cave. The briars kept her away. She rose onto her tiptoes, craning her neck. "What have you got in there?"

"Nothing."

"Clarence, I hear it."

She lifted the branches of the briars with the tips of her fingers and came around to the front of the cave.

"Oh my! Where did you get him?" I was pleased to see her excited, just like I had been.

"It's a girl, and she's mine."

"But where did you get her?"

"I found her in the woods."

"Where do you reckon she came from?"

"I figure she escaped from the circus. I'm going to keep her until they come back through town next year." By then, she'd be so used to me that she wouldn't want to live with a circus trainer anymore and I could keep her proper.

"She's beautiful. Can I pet her?" She moved her hand toward Cheetah.

"Careful! She's afraid of strangers. Is anyone with you?"

"No, I came out here by myself."

"You do that a lot, don't you?"

"I've seen you before too, Clarence," she replied. "It isn't like I'm weird or anything. I just like to be alone sometimes."

"I didn't say you were weird."

"What's her name?"

"Cheetah."

"Come here, Cheetah." Cheetah walked toward Elizabeth and sat down on the wooden crate next to her. "She's just wonderful," Elizabeth said. "Can she do any tricks?"

"She can follow me, and she does whatever I tell her to do," I said. "You have to swear not to tell anyone, especially not Hattie."

"Clarence, don't you think I'm smarter than that?"

"I just don't want anyone to hurt her."

"Why, if that old Henry got ahold of her, he might put her in a cage and torture her," she said. "Do your parents know about her?"

"I tried telling them but they didn't believe me. No one else knows but you."

Elizabeth stroked the top of Cheetah's head. "I got a biscuit in my pocket. Do you think she'd like some?" She reached in her pocket, unwrapped a napkin, pulled off a piece of biscuit and held it between her fingers. Cheetah grabbed it and stuck it in her mouth. "She's so cute. I wish I could have her."

Cheetah jumped back to my shoulder, carrying the rest of her biscuit. Elizabeth looked away from me and Cheetah and brushed her eyes up and down the sides of the cave like she was touching each piece of rock.

"I bet Indians lived here once. Wonder if we could see their drawings on the cave wall?"

"There aren't any Indian drawings on the wall."

"Maybe there are things buried in the cave."

"There ain't nothin' buried in the cave either."

"How do you know so much?" she asked.

" 'Cause I've been coming here a long time. I know all the caves and the old mine tunnels in these woods."

She ran her hand over the floor of the cave. The ground had sunk a bit and the dirt was loose over the hole where I kept my tin.

"This dirt is soft. Maybe there's something under here," she said.

"There ain't nothin' there. We'd better get out of here anyway," I said, pulling at Cheetah's collar. Elizabeth forgot what she'd been looking at and I breathed easier knowing she hadn't discovered my tin. I didn't want to give all my secrets away.

We pushed the briars against the cave opening.

"Goodbye, Cheetah." Elizabeth scratched the monkey's head. "I hope your place is safe, because with all the strikers roaming the woods, someone's bound to find you," she said.

"It's safe."

We reached the base of the hill by the dump and Elizabeth started picking through things. I sat down on a pile of old tires.

"I haven't been out here in a long time," she said.

"I used to come all the time."

"What did you do?" she asked.

"Looked for things. There's lots of good stuff people throw away."

"Really?"

We sat awhile, picking through bottles and tins.

"I saw you at the funeral," I told her.

"I saw you too."

"I guess you and Johnny were courting. You're probably pretty sad about him being killed and all."

"I am. Nobody should have to die like that."

"I guess not."

"You've been going to church all your life. Why do you reckon God let Johnny die?" she asked.

"I don't know."

"The preacher says that all things work for good, but I don't see any good in Johnny dying," she said.

"I don't think he means all things are good, just that God can make something good out of the bad. I've been years trying to figure out why I got born the way I did. But I stopped thinking about the why a while ago. I'm still waiting for him to make something good out of me, but it hasn't happened yet."

"Oh, you're funny, Clarence," she said, smiling.

"I am?"

"You are," she answered. "Thanks for letting me play with Cheetah. I won't tell, I promise," she said, and gave me a wink as she started down the road.

Chapter 25

Mother had been baking for a few days, preparing for the Fourth of July picnic. She made the best strawberry-rhubarb pie in the county, and that's not just me talking. There were lots of contests in everything from cooking to chopping wood, and Mother had come home with a blue ribbon the last three years in a row for her pie.

Most folks showed up before noon at Bagby Field and threw down their blankets near the river's edge. This year, we wondered if things would be different because of the strike. When we arrived, we saw a group of ladies arranging the table with fixings they had labored over but pretended to just whip up. There were baked beans, potato salad, deviled eggs, ham, pies, cobblers and cakes—everything you could ever want spread out on red-and-white checkered cloths laid over tables borrowed from the church. Once the food was laid out, you couldn't tell if it was made by the wife of a scab or a union man.

Off toward the river, there were huddles of men

who kept their distance from one another. Daddy's friends stood closer to the tables, and some I knew to be union men, like Sally's father, kept company by the riverside. They heaped large amounts of food on their plates and fell to eating when they got back to their groups. There was no fighting like we feared. The ladies mingled like they were at a church social. For them, the worst that could happen would be to take something home. Mother's pie was always good, but not even Daddy liked her carrot salad with raisins. We didn't have the heart to tell her, though, so Sterling had to finish it off for her sake and ours.

"I'll have to remember to make more of this next year, don't you think, Ezra?" she said, reclining on the blanket. "Why, people practically licked the bowl clean." Hattie almost wet her pants laughing.

There were lots of games, like egg tossing and three-legged races. Hattie and I were a team in a three-legged race but we collapsed midway. Sterling's favorite event was the watermelon-seed-spitting contest.

I hadn't noticed Clarence participating in games since most of them required a partner, but he jumped right up when they started the seed-spitting contest. Henry was an accomplished tobacco juice spitter and practiced as much as Sarah Perkins practiced her piano. He could spit from the side of his mouth, so I figured he'd be a shoo-in.

"Elizabeth," Mother called, "you and Hattie come away from there. That contest is for boys."

"We're just watching, Mother," I said.

"It isn't right for you to be watching boys spit," she said.

"It's only a game, and besides, we're cheering for Sterling."

The judges had marked a line where the contestants stood and laid a sheet about ten feet from there so they could see the seeds when they landed. It would be too hard to find them in the grass.

Sterling stepped up to the line and spat his first seed fifteen feet. Some boys liked to whirl their heads around or make funny faces, but Sterling was interested in the results, not in putting on a show. His second seed went only a few feet, but he was pleased with himself anyway. It was nice to see him enjoying himself for a while.

People started laughing when Clarence stepped up to the line. I felt my hands clench. It would have been nice for him to have Cheetah there, to have something to be proud of.

Clarence's first try dribbled out of his mouth and landed on his chin. Everyone laughed all the more. I put my hand over my mouth to keep anyone from seeing me giggle. I couldn't help myself. He stepped up again, his lips tight, his brow furrowed like it was the most important moment of his life. He hurled that seed close to twenty feet.

"Harelip is good for something," Henry yelled. "You ought to get a job spitting seeds, Henderson."

"You fool," Clarence's daddy said, coming up to him from behind, "a harelip spitting seeds belongs in a sideshow."

Clarence followed him back to the truck, where Mrs. Henderson sat in the front seat with her head bowed. Clarence didn't seem to mind the teasing as much as his daddy did. They left before the fireworks even started.

I felt about as sorry for Mrs. Henderson as I did for Clarence. She hardly ever smiled, and when she did, she never looked you in the eye, just like Clarence. She was wearing her rabbit sweater again. Mother said she wore it at the slightest hint of cold. She told me the story about it, and I aimed to write about it one day.

Mr. Henderson had had the widow Anderson knit him a pretty white angora sweater to give Mrs. Henderson the first Christmas they were married. He shot a snow-white rabbit and made a collar for the sweater with its fur. I couldn't imagine him doing such a thing. I never remembered seeing him smile. But everyone knew Mrs. Henderson was proud of the sweater; she wore it all the time.

I was sorry Clarence hadn't stayed. It turned out to be a fine evening, and the fireworks flashed red and gold and green, the prettiest I could remember. But the best part was that I didn't hear a word about the strike. Most of the men from Pittsburgh had gone home for the long weekend and wouldn't be back to camp for a while.

Sally Jennings came up after the fireworks to say hello. I had been avoiding her, though it wasn't really Sally that I was avoiding as much as it was talking about Johnny. There was so much going on that I figured I could watch everything and never have time to be sad unless someone like Sally was to come along and remind me.

"What have you been up to?" she asked.

"Not much."

"My mother has been taking me into Charleston one day a week for ballet lessons. I could show you some positions if you want to learn."

"Sure. That would be swell."

Sally had a natural grace about her, and I figured she would go to Hollywood someday. She loved dancing and never missed a Fred Astaire movie that came through town. She was an only child and got most things she wanted, except Sterling.

"I haven't seen much of your brother," she said.

"We haven't either. Don't take it personal or anything."

"Please tell him to watch out. My daddy says the union men have been quiet on account of the accident, but there's bound to be more trouble. I wouldn't want Sterling to get in the middle of it."

"I wouldn't either," I said. But I feared he was already there.

Chapter 26

"We shall not, we shall not be moved.
  We shall not, we shall not be moved.
  Just like a tree that's standing by the water,
  We shall not be moved."

I'd come home tired and stuffed full of food. Fireworks still flashed before my eyes.

"I got something I need to say to you children," Daddy said. "But you are going to have to give me your word that what I tell you will not leave this house."

Swearing of any kind made us well up with excitement.

"I won't tell," Hattie answered. Sterling and I looked at each other.

"Mr. Bagby has asked the union organizers from Pittsburgh and Logan County to move their camp. He has every right to, they're on his property. They refused. So tomorrow, we're going to have to move those men for him. I don't really want to do it, but it is within his rights."

"What do you mean?" asked Sterling

"We're going to take those tents down, bulldoze them if we have to."

"You can't do that!"

"Now, son, you listen here. It's within Mr. Bagby's rights to do it. Those men are bringing this trouble on themselves. Johnny Beasley would be alive right now if those men hadn't come. Let them go back to their families, where they belong."

"What if they try to shoot you? I heard those tents are full of guns," I said.

"We're going to roll in early enough that those men won't know what hit them. We've got some powerful machinery. It's not likely they'll be able to fight us. Don't worry, we'll be finished and be back out of town before the first shift rolls out at eight o'clock."

Sterling stood up to say something, looked straight at Daddy and stormed out of the room. I knew how he felt. It didn't seem right throwing men out of their only bed, and it was hard to think of Daddy doing something wrong like that anyhow.

I had an uneasy sleep. Every time I woke, I could still hear the creak of the rocker in the living room. I could smell Daddy's pipe and knew he must be worrying and wondering too.

When I finally fell asleep, morning had come. Hattie could hardly rouse me.

"Wake up, wake up, Elizabeth. Daddy's gone. He's gone to bulldoze those tents."

She went across the hall and knocked on Sterling's door. "Sterling, you'd better get up."

My head was heavy with dreams I fought hard to remember, but her gasp shook me fully awake. Sterling was gone. We pulled on our clothes as fast as we could and started for the door. Mother met us there.

"I knew he'd go," she said. "You girls are going to stay right here with me."

"Don't you think we should try to find him, try to bring him back?"

"It's probably too late for that. Sterling is out there wandering around. I don't need the worry of you too. This is dangerous business, men's business, and Sterling thinks he's a man."

Sterling had always had a destiny. Lots of boys probably thought they'd be president or some great general or athlete someday. Sterling's destiny was different. It wasn't that Hattie and I weren't special to Mother; we knew we were. But she had placed all her hopes and dreams in Sterling. It was like he had been chosen, like Jacob over Esau.

We sat on the front porch with our chins in our hands, straining to hear some noise somewhere. "It isn't fair," said Hattie. "It isn't right that we don't get to go and at least see what's going on."

"I can't bear to sit around and wait," I said. "Besides, I'm afraid Sterling is getting himself into trouble. We've got to try to keep him from it."

"Whose side are you on, Elizabeth?"

"I don't know," I said, looking away. "Daddy is a good man and he'd never do anything wrong. I think he ought to have a right to work. But Sterling is right too." I stood up. "I can't stand it anymore. I'm going into town. Are you going to come with me?"

Hattie jumped up too and we both ran down the road. We started laughing as soon as we were out of sight of the house.

"We're going to get in trouble," she said.

"I know we are, but I might have aged ten years if I had to sit there another minute."

Before we'd even gotten to the next house, we spotted Sterling running toward us. When he reached us, he put his hands on my shoulders to hold himself steady. He was staggering. We walked him back to the house while he caught his breath.

"What's wrong?" Mother came out on the porch.

"It was awful. The whole town has gone crazy. They headed in with those bulldozers just before day-break, knocking down everything in their path."

"Was anyone hurt?" she asked.

"They made such a racket getting to the camp that I think all the men were out. But they busted every-thing, their beds and chairs and tables, pushing them over the hillside. And the people in Widon were screaming like the dozers were coming for them next. Mrs. Hatcher was hysterical, pulling at her hair and crying, 'Don't touch my babies!' I couldn't stand to

155

watch it. It wasn't right," he said, shaking his head and grabbing a chair to sit down. "Those strikers are spitting mad, and I don't blame them."

"Let's hope they don't find out when your daddy and the rest of them are leaving the mine," Mother said.

Sterling pushed himself from his chair and went out to the back porch to sit, and we left him there. I headed for the woods as fast as I could. I wanted to see Cheetah and Clarence and talk to someone about all of this.

Chapter 27

Someone pounded on our door early in the morning. I pulled the curtain back to see one man standing on the porch and several more waiting in the back of a truck.

"Henderson, we need your help! The camp's been bulldozed," the man yelled through the door.

"I'll be right out," Pop yelled, and began stirring in the next room.

"The Braxton boy tells us they're quitting shift around eight o'clock. We're going to be ready for them," the man said.

I heard Pop grab his gun off the rack and watched him crawl in the back of the truck with the others.

Mama opened my door. "Get up, Clarence! I need your company or I'll worry myself to death. There's bound to be someone killed. Those men are powerful mad. God help us. Do you want me to fix you any breakfast, Clarence? It'll keep my mind off the trouble."

"I suppose."

But I dressed and made a sandwich out of the egg and toast so I could eat it on the run.

"Thanks, I think I'll go out walking."

"No you don't, Clarence! I told you that I need your company." She gave me a look that was familiar. Deep down she wanted to say no, to keep me home, where I was safe, but she couldn't deny me. I had grown past her size.

"Oh, go on," she said, "but don't you dare get near town or the mines."

I raced down past the dump to check on Cheetah first. She would be hungry.

When I arrived, she was waiting for me quietly, like she knew something was wrong. "You got to stay here for now, girl. It might be dangerous for you to come out. I'll be back when it's safe."

I stroked her back and let her climb for a while, long enough to stretch her legs.

It was nearing eight o'clock. I locked her up and headed for the other side of the hill, where I could see the road to the mine. At the base of the east side of the hill was the number-six mine, where most of the scabs worked. Around the corner, on the west side of the hill, a group of men stood clumped together talking. My pop was among them, looking over his shoulder. I knew him by the way he stood apart. He was never one to stand in a huddle.

They all had guns and began to climb up the steep hill opposite me, pulling at roots and the ground, heading straight for the old cookshack at the top. There must have been ten men waiting inside that shack, their rifles ready to bust out the windows and open fire in an ambush.

I stayed out of sight behind the thicket. From where I hid, I could see the scabs leaving the mine. Fifty men or so piled into cars, two or three into each one except the first one, which held only a lone driver.

I was waiting for them to start down the hill toward the bend in the road when I heard someone coming up behind me. I raised up behind the thicket just long enough to see Elizabeth walking up the path.

"Get down!" I whispered.

"What? Why?"

"The scabs are all about to get shot."

"What!"

"Faster, shhhh! If those guys over in that cookshack hear you, you could be shot too."

She ducked down and crawled on her hands and knees toward the thicket where I hid.

"We've got to stop it!" she said.

"My pop says that those scabs will deserve everything they get after bulldozing the tents."

"One of those scabs is my daddy. Maybe it wasn't right what they did, but killing is something different."

I knew my pop wouldn't understand, but I thought Elizabeth was right.

"We've got to stop it," she said again. As soon as she spoke, the cars started down the road. In the time it took us to turn our heads, black rifles poked out of the cookshack windows and a barrage of shots rang out loud as a clap of thunder. Men were yelling, "Get out of here!" "Go faster!" "Get down!" "Kill the damn scabs!" and then, a scream of pain. The first car stopped a second, then slowly rolled off the road into a ditch. It was Mr. Haley's. He was older, and not real friendly. At first I thought that maybe no one had wanted to ride with him, but then I realized that he had been the decoy. They must have known they were going to be ambushed. I started to shake. The rest of the cars sped by until they disappeared behind the bend in the road.

I looked over at Elizabeth. She was crouched down with her hands over her ears and tears running down her face.

"My daddy was down there!" she cried "Why didn't you stop them when you had the chance?"

"Do you think they would listen to me? Besides, it ain't me you should be angry with. It's Sterling. He told the union men about the shift change."

"He did not!" Her face was ashen.

"I heard it with my own ears."

"When?"

"This morning, when the men came to get my pop."

"I don't believe you! Sterling would never do a thing like that."

"Why don't you ask him?"

"You're an idiot, Clarence Henderson! Everyone always said you were retarded and now I know it's true!" She ran down the mountain right through a patch of briars, crying all the way. I crouched down into my thicket.

When the shooting stopped, the men eased themselves down the hillside, their guns still in position.

"He's dead," one said.

"By God, we've done it. They won't be messing with us anymore," said another.

"We'd have gotten 'em all if his car hadn't gone into the ditch."

"They got the message," I heard my pop say. "We're not going to be pushed around."

I had seen dead people before at funerals and wakes, but I had never watched a person die. I expected the scene to be bloody and awful, but the shot hit Mr. Haley so quickly that in an instant, he lay slumped and still over the steering wheel. In a matter of minutes it was over, and the men walked toward town like they'd just shot a fox in a henhouse.

I sat for a time just looking at him from the top of the

hill, his body so still and the road so empty and quiet. I crept down the hillside, my legs shaking as I neared the car. Bullet holes covered the side of the car and made it look like a tin can that had been used for target practice. Mr. Haley's hat had fallen over his forehead. As I got closer, I saw a trickle of blood coming from the side of his ear. I ran all the way home without stopping for breath.

Chapter 28

I ran down our road screaming, "Daddy! Daddy! Where's Daddy?" I burst out crying when he came out on the porch.

"You're all right! You're all right!" I threw my arms around him.

He leaned down and held me until I quieted.

"I saw those men shoot at the cars as they passed. I was so afraid you'd been killed."

"I made it, but Mr. Haley didn't."

"I know. I saw it. Weren't you scared?"

"Of course. We knew they were waiting for us somewhere. If Haley's car hadn't gone into that ditch, clearing the road for us to get by, they would have killed every last one of us. You shouldn't have been anywhere near that mine." I looked away from him.

Sterling had come out of the house to hear Daddy. "What's going to happen now?" he asked.

Daddy leaned against the porch railing, keeping me

close. His hands trembled as he stroked my hair. "The law has got to help us. They can't sit back and let people be killed."

"Why didn't the sheriff stop those men before they shot Mr. Haley?" I asked.

"For a long time, people said that the law was always on the owner's side. The sheriff has been making up for that by letting these union men carry guns and threaten those who didn't join them. But they've gone too far this time. The law is going to have to get involved."

Daddy put his arm around my waist and guided me inside.

"Are you all right, Sterling?" Daddy asked. "You look upset."

"I'm all right," he answered. Daddy saw me glare at him.

"Whatever is bothering you two, you better get it settled. We got enough tension in this house," Daddy said.

But I couldn't help it. I couldn't believe what Sterling had done. I had a mind to tell Daddy what Clarence had told me, but I just couldn't. It might hurt him more than Sterling, and Sterling was the one I was interested in hurting.

Sterling had gone out back to pull some spring onions for Mother.

"I know what you did," I told Sterling.

"What?" he said quietly.

"You told those men about the shift change."

"Who told you that?"

"Is it true?" Sterling looked down at the ground and used his sleeve to wipe the sweat from his forehead. He nodded.

"I didn't know what they were going to do. I swear I didn't, I swear it. I thought they were just going to scare the men like they'd done to Mr. Murphy. I didn't think they were really going to kill anyone." His eyes pleaded for my forgiveness.

"What about all their guns? You've been seeing them carry them everywhere they go. What did you think they were going to do with them?"

"It was stupid, I see that now. I shouldn't have said anything. I would never do anything to hurt Daddy. You know that."

"You killed that man! Aren't you ashamed, Sterling? That could have been Daddy!"

"Don't you think I know that!" He kicked at the dirt.

Angry as I was, I felt sorry for him just then. He had put himself on the line and the union men had let him down.

"You're not going to say anything to Daddy, are you?" His voice was soft and sheepish.

"I'll let you do that." I walked slowly back inside.

After supper the sheriff came by.

"I'm not going to have these men's blood on my hands," he said to Daddy. "This county's too big for me to stop this kind of thing unless I get some help. I aim to deputize some new men. Raise your right hand, Ezra. Do you swear to uphold the laws of this state and county and to abide by those laws, so help you God?" Daddy clicked his heels together and pulled his shoulders up to match the sheriff's.

"I do."

"You can carry a pistol to protect yourself," the sheriff said. "I aim to deputize any company man that wants it. They got a right to defend themselves. I am not going to let any man die without a fair fight."

With that, he got back into his car.

He drove through the county until three in the morning, until every man who continued to work for the mines was vested with the right to carry a pistol.

Sterling sat on the porch until late into the evening. He didn't even come in for supper, said he wasn't hungry.

"It's getting late," Daddy said to him hours after Hattie and I had gone to bed. "You aren't going to sleep out here, are you, son?"

I lay awake listening. "I can't stay here anymore," Sterling replied.

Daddy waited for Sterling to continue.

"I'm not one of you all anymore. I don't belong here," he said.

"How can you identify with a bunch of murdering thugs?"

"If you call those men defending their property a

bunch of murdering thugs, you might as well call me one too. I didn't pull the trigger but I . . ."

"What, son?" Daddy waited.

"I am as responsible as they are," he said.

"What! What do you mean?"

"I mean that I don't hold with the law deputizing the scabs and letting men be driven from their homes, men who are just trying to defend their rights. I can't take food or shelter from anyone who's hurting them," he said.

"You're making a big mistake."

"It's my mistake to make," he said.

"That it is."

I heard the door shut and Daddy settle into the bedroom. Sterling came in and stirred around, packing his things. He hadn't told Daddy the real reason he was leaving. Maybe he felt ashamed. The only thing I could hope for, for Sterling's sake, was that he really did believe the strikers were right.

Chapter 29

The town changed after the shooting. Friendliness was replaced by fear and suspicion. I saw Sally in town, but she only glanced my way without speaking. I raised my hand to wave at her but she turned away.

Mother saw my eyes brimming with tears. "Don't worry, Elizabeth. It's not her fault. Her father is a big union man. She can't very well be friendly to you right now."

"What if she never speaks to me?"

"She will. It'll straighten itself out in time."

I was lonely like I'd never been before. Just a few weeks ago, I had had Johnny and Sterling and Sally and even Clarence. And now they'd all been taken from me by the unions. If the union men hadn't come, none of this would have happened. If they hadn't come, I could have spent my summer like I always did, playing with Hattie and plotting trips to the swimming hole. Instead, we were practically confined to the house because of all of the men hanging around with guns. Mother wanted us within shouting distance at all times.

It had been a week since that awful day on the hill when Mr. Haley was killed. The sheriff had analyzed all the guns of the union men involved and found one that matched the bullet from Mr. Haley's body. Mr. Perkins was arrested. We heard talk of a big trial, but the judge said he couldn't get a fair jury in Clay so he was going to send for one in Braxton County. The whole thing didn't seem so fair to me. All of those union men had been there and any one of them could have killed Mr. Haley. But Mr. Perkins was probably going to have to pay for it. I knew someone should. Maybe it should be Sterling.

I couldn't bring myself to hate him, but I wanted to. I couldn't think of him without my heart racing and my teeth clenching. He had let himself get so caught up in the speeches that he didn't think for himself. I had always thought Sterling would be a leader. My friends at school admired his brains. Surely he could have talked those union men into something; he could have tried to keep them from hurting anyone. Maybe if they hadn't killed Mr. Haley, people would have been more sympathetic to them. Maybe they could have convinced a few more men to strike and the unions could actually have won. But now there was no hope of compromise.

I kept my mind focused on Sterling because I didn't want to think about what else had happened on that hill. Calling Clarence a retard was something Hattie would have done when she got mad, not me. I had to apologize. But saying I was sorry would be like pulling a nail out of a board. There would always be a hole left behind.

One afternoon, I snuck away to find him. I stuck a bag of nuts in my pocket for Cheetah. When I neared the cave, I heard Clarence talking to her. I stopped and listened, thinking about what to say.

"What are we going to do today, Cheetah? We could climb up on the hill and look for berries. You'd like that, wouldn't you?" Cheetah chittered like she understood. She ran from the top of her crate to his shoulder. Her hands were small and held Clarence's fingers like a child's. She spoke to him not with words but with jerky movements of her tail and deliberate chatterings. Her crate wasn't so much a cage anymore as a safe place. She was free when she was with him. She stayed close to him, drifting only to scale the high branches of the trees that he walked underneath. Clarence was just as free with her.

I stepped out in front of the cave so he would see me. He put his hand on Cheetah's shoulder and looked away.

"I'm so sorry, Clarence," I blurted out. "I'm sorry for calling you . . . for what I said to you. I never meant it. I was just so upset about Daddy and . . . I'm sorry."

He stared at the dust while I talked.

"I've heard it all before, anyway," he answered, stroking Cheetah's head with the back of his hand. "Is your daddy all right?"

"Yeah."

"That's good."

"And yours?"

"Same as always."

Mr. Haley didn't have a big family, but all the miners turned out for his funeral. The Bagbys showed up to pay their respects.

I didn't want to go to church on Sunday. But I wanted to lay down my cares. I wanted to stop worrying over why Johnny had died, or whether Daddy would get hurt, or how much pain I'd caused Clarence. I thought about what Mother had said about turning to God instead of away from him, so I put on my dress and carried my Bible and walked down the road to try to get right with God.

The preacher talked about the evil acts that union thugs perpetrated against law-abiding citizens. He called on all good Christians to separate themselves from evildoers. Mr. Pollson stood up halfway through the sermon and walked out. His wife followed, looking down as she passed through the aisle. But Pastor Greene kept on, his voice getting louder. Nothing the pastor said helped ease my troubles. So I stopped listening to him and listened to what God was saying to my heart. My hope was in His forgiveness. I had stopped being angry with God when I realized I needed Him. At the end of the service, we sang "Amazing Grace." We sang it all the time, but it never really meant much to me until that day.

Chapter 30

After she called me a retard, I wasn't mad at her like she thought I might be. That was the way people thought of me. I couldn't really expect her to feel different just because we shared the secret of Cheetah. She was honest as daylight and I knew she wouldn't betray that trust.

Elizabeth's company was something I didn't mind keeping. I had never had company before. But I held its thrill at a distance. I knew it could change like the value of scrip. I could be certain only of the noises of crickets in the summer night or the sound of water running over rocks in the creek. That is what I trusted.

Elizabeth snuck away almost every afternoon to visit Cheetah and me. She said her mother would worry if she was gone more than a couple hours. But we managed to take Cheetah for a good walk in that time. One day, we were trying to climb the hill over the mine, but her shoes were as slick as wet clay. She fell and scraped her arm.

"Grab my wrist, Clarence," she yelled.

Without thinking, I pulled her along the sandstone up to the top of the hill. My mama's touch was familiar, but it was the only one I knew until then. We walked around to the edge of the cave and I pulled back the briars, my heart reeling from the feel of her hand touching mine. We talked as we climbed, but all I remembered was that she had touched me and that it did not make her sick or feel like she had to wash her hands the way some girls did.

When we got to the top of the hill, we rested awhile. Elizabeth brought out some cookies wrapped in a napkin.

"Would you like one, Clarence? I know *you* would," she said, putting a piece in Cheetah's small black fingers.

"I guess." I popped one into my mouth.

"Sterling's been gone since the shooting."

"He has? Where's he been?"

"He's been sleeping in the union tents. Mother sets a place for him at the table every night in case he comes home. I wonder if he ever will. I miss him."

"Would your pop let him come home after what he did?"

"I don't think there's anything any of us could do that would make Daddy mad enough to keep us from coming home. Even so, I don't think he knows that Sterling was the one who told the men about the shift change. He'd be pretty upset if he did. I talked to Sterling about it. He told me he didn't know what was going to happen. He never expected anyone would get hurt."

"You mean he didn't know they were going to try to kill somebody?"

"He thought they'd scare the miners, that's all. He just wanted to do something important, something to help the unions."

"My pop thinks they're right too."

"What do you think, Clarence?"

"I've been listening to my pop complain about the mines for so long, I wouldn't mind things being different for him. It doesn't matter much to me 'cause I'm never going to work there."

"What are you going to do?

"Go to college."

"You are?"

"My mama is saving money for me to go."

"Well, Clarence, I think that would be a mighty fine thing for you to do. I hope to go too, to become a teacher."

"You'd be a good teacher."

"Do you really think so?"

"Sure, you're smart and patient."

She smiled. "Do you know what you'd like to do?"

"I like animals. I might want to be a veterinarian."

"You'd be a great veterinarian."

"Really?"

"Sure, you're smart and patient."

"Thanks." We both laughed. "Let's do something fun," I said. "There's a great vine up on the side of the hill. Let's climb it."

"Okay," she said.

I ran way ahead of her and hid behind the giant tree at the top of the hill.

"Clarence, where did you run off to?"

"Roar!" I leapt out behind her.

"Ahhh!"

"I thought you weren't afraid?"

"Not until you screamed!"

The vine had grown twisted around some tree branches. I grabbed it and crawled to the top.

"Clarence, no wonder you and Cheetah became close. You're practically a monkey yourself. I just hope you don't kill yourself up there!"

"I do this all the time. Come on up."

"I could never get up there."

"I'll lift you."

"I might fall."

"I'll hold you."

"Well, all right." She grabbed at the base of the vine and I held on tight to the branch with my legs. Cheetah was up in the tree beside me, chirping. She sounded more nervous than Elizabeth.

I swung down and offered her my hand. She

grabbed it while I shinnied back to the top, pulling her along.

"Clarence, don't let go of me."

"I won't."

Her hands gripped the branch and she hoisted herself over the top of it and sat.

"Whew! Wow. It's beautiful up here. Look, you can see all the way over the side of the mountain."

"I know," I answered.

"Wouldn't it be great to have a tree house up here? Maybe we should build one for Cheetah."

"You wouldn't mind climbing the tree every day to see her?"

"It might be a little hard unless you were here to help me. Clarence, you're—you're smarter than I thought," she stammered. "It isn't that I thought you were dumb, it's just that—I guess I hadn't really talked to you before."

"Thanks. I guess," I said.

"You know a lot about the woods."

"I should. I spend so much time here. If you like this spot, I got another one I'll show you tomorrow. It's even higher than this one. You have to climb over two giant rocks to get to it."

"I promised I would help my mother with the laundry tomorrow."

"Maybe some other time." I feared I had been too anxious.

"Do you want to know something, Clarence?"

"I guess."

"You have to swear not to tell anyone," she said, her eyes wide and serious. "Or you don't have to swear, 'cause it says not to swear in the Bible, but you do have to promise 'cause I never told anyone before now."

Henry had told me things he said he had never once told anyone, but I didn't believe him. Henry told everything more than once. I didn't think I had ever really had a real secret of someone else's to keep before.

"I swear."

"It's about Johnny," she said.

"You must be pretty upset about him dying."

"I wish you wouldn't say that, at least not to me," she said.

I felt bad. I'd said the wrong thing.

"I mean, of course I'm sad. It's just that, while he was my friend and all—well, I guess he was my boyfriend—I didn't love him the way everyone thinks. I was thinking about breaking it off with him."

I must have looked at her funny 'cause then she started crying.

"Oh, Clarence, I shouldn't have told you. Isn't it awful to speak about a dead person that way, I mean to say that you didn't love them when everybody thinks you did? I just can't bear all these people feeling so sorry for me."

"I didn't like him that much. He was all the time teasing me."

"I heard him once. But don't hold it against him. He really wasn't so bad. You won't tell anyone, though, will you, Clarence?"

"I won't."

We climbed down slowly. I went first and helped her ease herself down. We walked on a ways in silence. Cheetah sat on my shoulder.

"Clarence, don't you worry that someone will find Cheetah out here?"

"No one knows about the cave but me and you."

"But Clarence, if someone hears her, they're bound to find it. The briars you put up are only going to keep people from discovering the cave if it's all quiet, but someone is going to cut through them if they hear her calling inside."

"What can we do?"

Elizabeth thought for a moment. "What about that ravine between your house and mine? We could keep her there."

"Doesn't your daddy's hound wander down there?"

"He's too old. He doesn't go past the front porch anymore."

The ravine was dark and rocky and full of mountain laurel and ferns that crept down the hillside along the small stream thick with crawdads.

We decided to build a little box out of some scrap wood at the dump and move Cheetah as soon as we could.

*   *   *

We'd take Cheetah with us and let her wander around while we built her new cage, hammering as the train passed so no one would hear us.

"Clarence," Elizabeth said, "what would happen if someone did find Cheetah?"

"Well, I don't know. I'm going to tell people about her anyway. I was thinking of taking her to the county fair in a few weeks."

"Why would you want to do a thing like that?"

"I just do," I told her. "I want people to see her and know that she's mine."

I imagined what it would be like walking to the fair with her on my shoulders and maybe Elizabeth with us, to say, "Howdy, Jacob Anderson," while he stood there with his prize Holstein, thinking she was something special until he got a look at us.

Elizabeth and I made her cage bigger this time and covered it up with branches and vines so no one would see it right away. "There you go, girl." I laid some nuts in her cage, feeling happy.

180

Chapter 31

The strike lasted longer than anyone had expected. Mr. Bagby dug in his heels and had just about enough working men to keep the mines running. But he was losing a big contract on account of not being able to meet the larger orders.

Daddy got paid for extra time and gave some food to the church since many of our neighbors were going without. Daddy thought that once Sterling got hungry, he would head home. He didn't. I hated to admit it, but I missed him. I can't say I missed his smile or his laugh because I hadn't seen or heard those for a while. Instead, I missed the sound of his knife hitting wood. I missed the look of his slumped figure as he sat contemplating on the back porch. I got a taste of what life might be like if he went away to college. It made me think of what it must have been like all the time for Johnny's family, the presence of empty space that only he could fill.

Our dinners were quiet, and Mother always tried to find something for us to talk about. "Have you girls seen anything unusual around my chicken coop?" she asked one night. "Something is stealing the eggs. I looked hard for coon prints but haven't seen a one. You children watch out for it now. Ezra, maybe you better set another trap for whatever is getting my eggs," she said. I couldn't tell if that was Mother just making conversation or if something was really after her eggs.

"I hope that fox isn't back," Grandma said.

"If it is," Mother said, "that red fox would make a very fine stole." She winked at Daddy.

"Mother, don't let Daddy shoot him. He's so pretty, and he's got a family too. I saw the kittens last spring. They were all gray with red tails," Hattie said.

"If he doesn't stop stealing my eggs, there'll be no eggs in the morning and no birthday cake or hotcakes for you, my dear," Mother replied.

"Oh," Hattie said. She had an insatiable sweet tooth.

"I wouldn't be surprised if it was the strikers," Daddy said. "I heard tell they were running out of supplies. You girls be extra careful in the woods and if you hear shooting, you get yourselves home."

"Yes sir," I answered. Hattie looked at me, worried.

Angela and her mother were supposed to come by that evening to drop off some sewing patterns for Mother. Mother earned extra money on the side making dresses and skirts.

When they arrived, I went out to the front porch while Mother pinned Angela's dresses. I didn't feel like watching Angela parade around like a model. She came out to find me when they were finished, smiling like I'd be so excited to see her. "Have you seen much of Sally this summer?"

"I saw her in town, but she doesn't come over anymore because of the strike, seeing that our fathers are on opposite sides."

"I got the same problem. I miss her," she said.

"I do too."

"I haven't seen much of you either," she said. "Mother doesn't like us to go far. Hattie comes to the swimming hole some, but you never do."

"I guess I've been busy."

"Doing what?" she asked. I was quiet. "Hattie tells me you've been hanging out with Clarence Henderson. You'd better stop hanging around him all the time, just you and him alone. People are going to think something is going on," she said, and paused. I was thinking about what to say when she blurted out, "I mean, I know it's not. You would never be interested in a boy like him. It's just that I hope you're not counting on walking to school with him or anything. No one is going to go out with you with him hanging around."

"I thought your mama taught you better than that," I said.

"Being kind is one thing. Being friends is altogether different. It's okay to be nice to Clarence, I've

183

got no quarrel with that. But you're acting like he ain't—well, ain't what he is."

"And what is that, Angela?"

"He's a freak, that's what he is," she said, and turned her face sour.

"Clarence is my friend, Angela, and he's always going to be. If you don't like that then you can find yourself another girlfriend."

I was more startled by my own words than hers. I got up and stomped off the porch. I had finally stood up for him.

Chapter 32

"I got something for you to do tonight," Pop said when I came back from the woods.

"There's a meeting tonight in Clay, and I want you to come."

"Don't take him," Mama said, appearing from the kitchen.

"I need him," Pop said. "He's going to help us tonight."

"Doing what?" I asked.

"I don't want him in danger!" Mama said.

"We're all in trouble, woman. This strike ain't going anywhere. That's why we're meeting, and he's going to be our lookout. No one would think he'd be up to anything. Right, boy?" He slapped the back of my head. "Come on, get in the truck."

It was the first thing he'd asked me to do that wasn't a chore. I was going to be on a regular spy mission, like in the movies.

"Why are we going all the way to Clay when most of the strikers live in Widon?"

"Any meeting of more than two people brings the sheriff out in the company town. But no one can stop us from meeting in Clay," Pop answered.

When we got to Clay, we hopped out of the truck and Pop surveyed the street like he hadn't seen it before.

"You sit over there," he said, pointing to a bench across the street from the hotel. "If you see someone heading for the hotel, whistle real loud." Then he turned and went in the front door.

I could see men through the window, four in all, playing cards and drinking. After a while, it started to rain, so I crossed the street to stand under the hotel's awning.

Their whispers traveled out the open window, along with the chink of the coins they threw against the table.

"So, Akeley, what's a hotel owner like you care about the strike?" I heard my pop say.

"My father was killed in a mine war long ago. I feel like I owe it to him to help you men out any way I can."

I recognized Mr. Hudson from his hat. He never took it off, even inside. Mama said it wasn't polite, but Pop said he was just ashamed of being bald. He was real big in the unions.

"Boys, we been holding that camp for two months and haven't gotten one inch closer to making any deals. Nothing is going to happen down here until something big happens. We got to put some pressure on Bagby," Mr. Hudson said.

"What kinda pressure you talking about?" I heard Pop ask.

Mr. Hudson hesitated. "I don't want no cowards, and I know that you men aren't, but this is the first time we're going to be putting our lives on the line for what is right."

"They're loading a thousand tons of coal out of that number-six mine every day," Mr. Hudson continued. "That's just enough to keep them in business. We just about closed down the number-four mine, so they aren't making money from that. We did a rundown of all the men at number six and figure none of them are going to go union. We got to keep them from loading that coal, and we ain't going to do it by talking either."

"I don't want no more blood on my hands," Pop said.

"Me either," said Mr. Akeley.

"I'm not talking about killing, I'm talking about shutting down a mine." Mr. Hudson was calm and deliberate. The men were all quiet.

"There's a vent shaft for the number six at the back of Beaver Hollow. They've got guards everywhere else, but if we could get some men down into the mine when no one was there, we could blow that thing and stop any work."

"But where are we going to work when the strike is over?" Pop asked.

"By then, all the debris will be cleared away. I'm not talking about destroying the mine altogether, just shutting it down long enough to force them to the table. A little dynamite will stop them just long enough for us to get a settlement," Mr. Hudson answered firmly. "Let me put it to you directly. Which of you gentlemen is man enough to pull this off?"

"I am." It was Pop.

I was proud of my pop just then.

They lowered their voices so that I couldn't hear any more.

The storm had passed and been replaced by a high half-moon peeking through thinned gray clouds. I figured it was near midnight before Pop finally came out of the hotel. He didn't say goodbye to anyone. I followed him to the truck and we drove home. Without saying a word, he sighed and looked over at me in a way I'd never seen him look before. He seemed scared.

Chapter 33

"Wake up, Clarence. You're not going to sleep all day, are you?" Mama asked.

"What time is it?"

"Close to noon. Your pop must have wore you out at the meeting last night."

I pulled on my pants, laced up my shoes and started for the door. If I didn't feed Cheetah soon, she'd make a big racket.

"Now, where are you going in such a hurry? You didn't even eat your breakfast."

I stepped back inside to grab a piece of bread and headed out the door.

"Don't be gone long—you've got chores to do!"

As I neared the ravine where we'd moved Cheetah's cage, I heard voices. I stopped short and hid behind an elm tree. I poked my head out long enough to glimpse Sterling and a couple of men I'd seen hanging around the camp. One of the men held a gun, and Sterling stood admiring it.

"I bet I could get me a scab from a hundred yards," the man said.

"Those scabs are easy 'cause they're so yellow," another laughed.

"Hey, watch out. Sterling might get mad since his daddy is a scab." The two men wrinkled their faces in laughter. One raised the gun long enough to squeeze off a shot. Two cans they had set up for target practice went pinging over the side of the hill.

"That ain't so bad," Sterling said. "I'm getting hungry. See if you can take that squirrel out of that tree," he said, gesturing upward.

"That ain't no squirrel," the man said, "that's a possum."

"What's a possum doing up there in the daytime?"

"Shoot it and see," the other said.

"Stop!" I screamed just as the gun went off.

"No! No!" I yelled, rushing toward the place where I heard the thud of her body hitting the ground. The men turned to follow me.

I found her body, limp against the base of the tree. Her eyes were fixed ahead.

"Oh my God!" Sterling said. "You shot a monkey."

"Don't tell me she belonged to this half-wit?" the man said, pointing to me.

I touched her fur and tried to rouse her, but she lay still. "You killed her!" I yelled.

"You fool!" one of the men said to the shooter. "We probably could have sold it for something."

I picked up her body and raced over the hill through briars and poison ivy patches. I wanted to run as far as I could. I wanted to run until I died.

Hattie and I were sitting on the porch thinking about what we were going to do when we heard the shooting. We didn't think much of it until we saw Sterling coming up the road. My heart leapt at seeing his figure.

Daddy was fiddling with the car. He wiped his hand with a rag and laid it on Sterling's back. "It's good to see you, son." Sterling's lips turned up in a slight smile, relieved at Daddy's touch. But he shifted his weight nervously from foot to foot.

"I heard some shooting," Daddy said. "Is everything all right?"

"We were just down near the ravine looking for something to eat."

"Whose rifle were you using?" Daddy asked.

"One of the strikers had it." Sterling stood there a moment and I watched him from the porch. "There was an animal in the tree. We thought it was a squirrel, but it wasn't."

Daddy stopped to look at him. "What was it?"

"A monkey. I don't know where it came from. I

figure it was from the circus or something. One of the men shot it." He paused. "Clarence Henderson came up and yelled at us. He said it was his."

"What!" I cried.

"Elizabeth?" Mother asked.

"Sterling and those stupid strikers did an awful thing, the worst thing in the world," I yelled. "They killed Clarence's monkey. Oh, why did you do it? Why?"

I rushed over to Sterling and pounded my fists against his chest. "You killed her, you idiot! You killed her!"

"We didn't know it was a monkey! We needed food!" he protested.

"She was Clarence's pride and joy!" I wailed.

Daddy tried to hold me back.

"Calm down," Sterling pleaded. "It was only a monkey."

"You don't understand. Mother, make him understand. It wasn't just Clarence's monkey, it was all he had." I started to sob.

"I promise we wouldn't have done it if we'd known," Sterling said. Mother put her arm around him.

"What did you do with it?" Mother asked.

"Clarence saw us. He took it."

"Why didn't they tell me about the monkey?" Hattie asked. "How come I never knew?" No one paid attention to her.

I sat on the porch crying, my face in my hands. What could I do? There was no way to get Clarence another monkey like we might have done if it had been a cat.

"Sterling, you go over to the Hendersons' and apologize to the boy and his parents," Daddy said. "And Elizabeth, you go help him." He looked at me. "You'll know how to talk to the boy."

Daddy never called Clarence by his name.

We thought we'd wait until after supper to give Clarence a chance to get home. Mother busied herself in the kitchen while Sterling sat on the porch. I stood behind him, thinking. He wore his recklessness in his thin frame, but his tired heart was still visible to me. The shock at what he had done had eased some, and I even felt glad to have him home, despite the reasons. When we sat down to eat, Sterling gulped what food Mother set before him. The minute we were finished, we set off for the Hendersons'.

We saw laundry hanging out back and glimpsed Mrs. Henderson working there. We knocked on the door, half hoping no one would answer. But Mr. Henderson did.

"Hello, Mr. Henderson. I wanted to talk to Clarence."

"Something wrong, Sterling?" He ignored me. "My boy caused any trouble?"

"No sir, I was the one that caused the trouble. Some friends and I shot Clarence's monkey by accident.

I mean, we shot it on purpose, but we didn't know what it was. It's not like you see lots of monkeys in Clay."

"What are you talking about, Clarence's monkey?"

"Clarence had been keeping a monkey in the woods for a couple of months," I said. "He found it at the dump. It must have escaped from the circus."

"I've never heard of such a thing," he answered.

Mrs. Henderson came to the door wearing a worried look.

"Where is he?" his daddy asked.

"He ran off around lunch and didn't come back for supper. What's this about?" Mrs. Henderson said.

"Sterling tells me Clarence has been keeping a monkey in the woods."

"Now, that's a silly thing," said Mrs. Henderson. "Where would a boy like Clarence get a monkey?" She paused, her eyebrows furrowed. "Addison, don't you remember, he told us that once, but we didn't believe him?"

"It doesn't matter now. Sterling says he kilt it."

Sterling broke in, his voice cracking. "I couldn't tell what it was, thought maybe it was a squirrel or something. Honest."

"I'll tell him when he comes home," Mr. Henderson said, not seeming to grasp the importance of everything.

"Thank you for letting us know," said Mrs. Henderson, trying to be pleasant, as she shut the door.

Sterling and I walked home in silence. I closed my eyes to pray for Clarence and opened them every few feet to keep from stumbling and to make sure Sterling was beside me. He was, and he was praying too, I could tell. We sat down on the porch steps.

"I done wrong, Elizabeth. First Mr. Haley and now this," he said. "What am I going to do?"

"I think we should try to find Clarence."

"Do you know where he might be?"

"I have an idea." Sterling ran inside to grab a flashlight.

"Let's go," he said, and we lit out down the road for the woods.

Chapter 34

Of all the days for Cheetah to get out of her cage, why had it been this one? It wasn't fair. It was the only day that I'd slept late all summer. Why was I born so cursed?

I carried her body to the cave and laid it gently where I'd kept her crate.

Why hadn't I stopped them earlier? What had I been afraid of? So what if they'd called me a name? At least I'd have had her, at least she'd have been alive! I went over it dozens of times. But it didn't matter. She was gone.

I thought of her cage and how it would sit empty. Maybe some other animal would build a nest in it.

And what would I do now? It seemed that I had had Cheetah for a long time. I had forgotten what it was like to be lonely. I couldn't stand the thought of being without her. It wasn't just Cheetah; it was Elizabeth too. Why would she want to come around anymore if Cheetah wasn't there? And Henry would get word of what happened and tell everyone about me keeping a monkey in the woods and how Sterling's union buddy had killed it and how I had cried. It would only make me seem more of a fool.

There was a knot in my stomach from hunger, but I didn't want to go home. I didn't want to tell anyone, not even Mama. And I knew Pop would only be mad at me for keeping a monkey. I took my knife and began digging in the soft dirt. Her body had stiffened already. I stroked her fur and curled her up like she was sleeping. I pushed the dirt back over her until it made a small mound. I fashioned a cross with some sticks and tied them together with grass. When I finished, I lay down beside her grave and tried to close my eyes. But the moon was rising low and big, and I couldn't sleep.

Instead, I gazed out of the cave. I could see all the way to the front of the mine. I heard a couple men laughing and saw the flicker of their lantern shining on some bottles and cards between them.

It was quiet except for their voices and occasional fits of deep laughter. I was about ready to lay my head back again when I spotted the beam of a flashlight coming up the side of the road. I wondered who it was and why they weren't driving. Just when they neared the mine, they shut off their light. But the moonlight gave me a glimpse of them moving through the trees and up the side of the mine.

That was when I remembered about the meeting the night before. Tonight was the night that something big was supposed to happen, and Pop was supposed to do it. For a couple seconds, the flashlight came on again, long enough for me to see a man standing beside the upper mine shaft. I wasn't sure, but I thought it might be him. He disappeared into the mountain with the light. Minutes later, a huge flash of fire shot out from the side of the mountain. In an instant an explosion rocked the cave. I screamed and the siren blew.

The guards were grabbing their bottles and clearing off the table. I jumped out of the cave and ran to the shaft, ignoring the branches that slashed at my face. When I arrived, dirt was spilling out of the top of the opening. Pop's flashlight was there. I grabbed it and shined it as far down the hole as I could. There was nothing but dust hanging heavy in the air.

"Pop, Pop, can you hear me?" I got down on my hands and knees and dropped myself down into the shaft.

"Pop!" I cried. I heard a faint cough.

"Pop, is that you?"

"Help!" he screamed. "My arm is busted. I can't move. Somebody help me!"

"Pop, can you hear me? It's me," I said.

"Clarence? Clarence, you gotta get help. My arm is aching something awful and the dust is so thick I can barely breathe."

"I'll get you out, Pop."

"You can't get me out. Go get help!"

I fumbled around until I felt a rock. I grabbed it and started digging away at the dirt. I heard the rumbling of the mountain, like the low growl of a bear. I didn't have much time.

Chapter 35

We stayed on the road to the mine as far as we could. The night's shadows played tricks on me.

"I thought you knew where he might be," Sterling said.

"I think I know, I just can't find it." I started off the road in another direction.

"We've tried that path, remember?" Sterling said.

"I'm sorry. That looked like the tree where I usually turn." I begged the night to help us find him.

"We're practically to the mine. I see the lights up ahead," Sterling said.

"We've gone too far," I said. Then we heard an explosion that made the road beneath us rumble.

"What was that!" I screamed.

"The mine!"

My heart was racing and my legs struggled to keep up with Sterling. The siren blew, making us run even faster. When we got to the face of the mine, no one was there. The guards' table was abandoned.

"What's going on? Where is everybody?" Sterling yelled to the mountain.

"Up here!" We heard a faint cry.

We raced up the hill, looking for anyone or any sign of what had happened. Sterling's light flashed on an area thick with dust.

"Help!" We heard a cry inside the mine.

"Clarence?"

"It's my pop, he's hurt bad. I got to get him out of here!" Clarence's feet dangled out the back of the hole.

"Come out, Clarence. Let me see what I can do," Sterling said.

"What are you going to do? Shoot him too?"

"Come on, Clarence. Let me help. I might be able to do something."

Clarence backed out on his knees. "There's a rock blocking the hole. I tried to move it, but I can't."

"Maybe I can. You two go get help." Sterling crawled into the dark hole.

Clarence took off running, but I peered into the tunnel. "Be careful. Sterling . . . ? Sterling! Oh! Be careful!" Then I ran.

* * *

201

Daddy's headlights flashed on me as I ran full force along the road. Hattie had jumped in the back of Daddy's truck when they'd heard the explosion.

"What happened?" Daddy yelled. I leaned up against the truck, too out of breath to speak.

"It's Addie Henderson. He's trapped," I panted. "We've got to get help—equipment, shovels. Sterling went in to get him."

"What in the world was Addie Henderson doing at the mine?"

Daddy knew it was nothing good. We drove to another mine, where we grabbed shovels and lanterns and threw them in the truck. "Hurry!" I screamed. When we got there, Daddy and I rushed up the hill with our shovels. The guards followed with rakes and lanterns. Hattie climbed up behind us. It was strangely quiet.

"Are you sure this is where he is?" Daddy asked.

"Yes, yes!"

"Sterling! Clarence!" Daddy crawled on his hands and knees as far as he could into the shaft.

There were groans from deep within the mountain, and we knew it wasn't going to hold back much longer.

"Addison, can you hear me?" Daddy cried. He backed out, with Sterling just behind him.

"I tried getting to him but I just couldn't move the rock," Sterling said, his face smeared with dirt and tears. "Addie stopped answering me a little while ago."

He picked up a shovel and tried digging from another side.

"Stay away from there, son. You might cause it to cave in."

"Where's Clarence?" I asked.

"I don't know," Sterling said. "I thought he went with you." I looked around, helpless. Hattie and I put our arms around each other and waited. I couldn't stop praying even to breathe.

The hillside became dotted with huddles of lanterns as more and more men came to help, miners and strikers carrying shovels and wearing hard hats. But as they approached, they understood that the threat from the weakened shaft was too serious for anyone else to go in. We were all waiting, whispering, listening to the scraping of a shovel deep within the hole where Daddy had thrown himself after Mr. Henderson. Sterling crouched at his feet, shining a light for him to see. I could not take my eyes off that opening in the shaft. All of a sudden we felt a tremor beneath our feet. My knees buckled under me when the mountain began roaring. A host of watchers ran down the mountain in terror. The ground shifted under our feet, sending a plume of dirt out the hole where Daddy had gone.

"Daddy!" I cried, and crawled to the edge to see him.

"Stand back, Elizabeth!" someone yelled. "Ezra, come out. There's nothing you can do anymore."

The dirt was pouring in all around. As soon as Daddy

lifted his head from the hole, earth fell in such a heavy rain that we all knew Mr. Henderson had been buried.

Hattie started screaming, "No! No! Please, someone help him!" Sterling stood shaking.

Daddy grabbed me tight and held me long after the mountain had stopped. *What will we tell Clarence?* I thought. *What will we tell him now?*

We were still standing there, hoping against hope, when we saw Mother climbing up the hillside.

"What's happened?" she asked, panting.

"It's Addie Henderson. He's been buried," Daddy said.

"Then I must have just seen a ghost," she said.

"What do you mean?" I asked.

"He and Clarence climbed out the back shaft. They're down in the truck, getting cleaned up. Addie's arm is messed up pretty good."

Sterling took off running over the hill and Hattie and I followed, tears streaming down our faces.

There was a crowd of people gathered around them. Sterling broke through. "We thought you'd been killed."

"I didn't think I was going to make it either," Mr. Henderson answered.

"Your arm doesn't look so good."

"It could have been a lot worse if it hadn't been for Clarence."

Daddy had caught up with us at the bottom of the hill. "How did you get him out, Clarence?"

"There was an old shaft up on the hill. I knew it might be worth a try."

"That's good thinking," Daddy said.

"Clarence Henderson!" I said, and kissed him on the cheek. He jumped away. His mother laughed and so did he.

Addie Henderson put his hand on his shoulder. "You could have been kilt."

"I'm too smart for that," he replied. And he was.

Chapter 36

A few days after the accident, Mother sent Sterling and me over to the Hendersons' with a triple-layer cake she'd baked to help with Mr. Henderson's recovery.

Clarence was on the front porch with a brand-new fishing pole from his pop. He was glad to see us and show Sterling his new pole. They made plans to go fishing that afternoon. He smiled wide and didn't try to cover his mouth the whole time we were there. "Want to come fishing with us?" He knew I didn't like fishing. He knew as much about me as anyone. I smiled at the thought.

"I'd rather go climb that tree up on the hill," I answered.

"What tree is that?" Sterling asked.

Clarence winked at me. "I'll meet you there in the morning."

* * *

After the accident, the strike petered out. Many of the union men went back home. Mr. Bagby waited until Mr. Henderson's arm healed to press charges against him. He ended up spending a few months in jail for his part in the explosion.

Most of the strikers didn't go back to work in the mines. Sterling was the exception. Daddy said he was proud to have Sterling working alongside him, even after the trouble he'd caused. "I have a lot of respect for a man who acts on what he believes, even if I disagree with him."

That spring, Sterling didn't take the scholarship Mr. Bagby offered him. He said he'd rather pay his own way. He went to college in Huntington and worked summers to pay for his tuition. He never gave up on his union hopes either.

Bagby sold out a few years later and the unions came in, offering pensions to everybody. But by that time, Sterling had joined the army.

My last two years in high school, I worked on my writing and didn't go to any dances. Sally and Angela told me all about them as if I'd want to know, but I didn't.

I saw more of Clarence in high school. We were in a few of the same classes and studied together sometimes. He was much better at algebra than I was. He joined a 4-H club and raised a pig for the fair. I don't think the boys teased him as much, or if they did, he didn't seem to be as bothered by it. We graduated the same year and had his folks over after the ceremony for some cake.

Mrs. Henderson wore her angora sweater and even had a sip of champagne. "I knew in my heart he was going to make it. That's why I saved those coins all these years," she said. His pop kept saying, "It's the darnedest thing, that boy going off to college." Clarence left for school soon after that, and I went to college on the Bagby scholarship.

Clarence set his sights on becoming a vet and went to Kentucky to do it. Some years later, he wrote to me to tell me he was coming back to find work in Clay and that he was particularly interested in that piece of land high on the hill where so many of my stories had found their beginning.

I don't remember much else about that summer. All summers seemed to get shorter as I got older. The union formed while I was off at college. Mama had the *Clay Free Press* sent to my dorm to make me feel at home. It helped me keep track of the world I'd left behind.

I read where Hattie married Elmer Atkinson, whom I recall she had sworn she hated, and settled in downtown Clay. Sterling joined the army after college, but I heard awhile back that he had returned to teach at the high school.

It was Elizabeth I wanted most to read about. When she first left town to go to college, she received several school honors. She graduated from college Phi Beta Kappa and entered graduate school in Charleston to study English. After that she dropped from the papers for a while. Then one day there was a photograph of her with a book she'd published about our town. She said writing it had made her want to come back. Reading it made me want to go back too. By then, I had my own veterinary practice in Kentucky, but I wrote to tell her I would be interested in settling that overgrown farm high on the hill across from where she used to sit.

About the Author

Julie Baker grew up in West Virginia, where she listened to many stories of the mine wars. She now lives in Charlottesville, Virginia, with her husband, Jonathan, and five children. She spends her time teaching English, doing laundry, and learning how to raise sheep and grow pawpaws.